# SNARE

## When the Adulteress Hunts

# SNARE

## When the Adulteress Hunts

Tiffany Buckner

Anointed Fire House Publishing

www.anointedfirehouse.com

United States Copyright Office

© 2015, Snare: When the Adulteress Hunts

Author: Tiffany Buckner

info@anointedfire.com

Published by Anointed Fire™ House

Website: www.anointedfirehouse.com

ISBN-13: 978-0692570531

ISBN-10: 0692570535

# Dedication

I dedicate this book back to the Author and Finisher of my faith, Jesus Christ. I am forever grateful to you for the sacrifice you made on the cross for me. I declare that you, Jesus Christ, are Lord.

# Table of Contents

*"In the same way husbands should love their wives as their own bodies. He who loves his wife loves himself. "*
(Ephesians 5:28/ ESV)

## Chapter 1

# The Beginning of the End

It was three in the morning and Naomi had just woken up suddenly. She stretched her arm across the bed, only to see that Jeff, her husband, still hadn't come home. Jeff's side of the bed was cold and the room felt cold and empty. Naomi picked up Jeff's pillow and covered her face with it as she wept. She muzzled her face and screamed as loud as she could into the pillow. The pain was agonizing and Naomi was out of ideas as to what she could do to save her marriage. This was the tenth time that Jeff hadn't come home. As a matter of fact, he'd started an argument the previous night and left. To make matters worse, the argument wasn't one that merited Jeff's over-the-top reaction. Jeff had come home from work, and after noticing his wife's new hairstyle, he'd jokingly compared her to a shaved llama. Naomi was offended, so she got up from the dinner table, went into the bedroom and closed the door. Instead of coming to check on his wife or apologize for his actions, Jeff grabbed his keys and left. Before leaving, he yelled to his wife that he was tired of her attitude.

Naomi removed the pillow from her face as she flipped her body over to face Jeff's side of the bed. She squeezed Jeff's pillow tightly, closed her eyes and pretended that he was lying next to her. "You were my everything," she said. "How could you hurt me like this? I've been there for you, Jeff and you know it. I stood by your side when your family turned their backs on you. I stood by you when you had no job, plus, I gave you two beautiful children. How could you hurt me, Jeff? I upset my mother by sticking with you after you took Michelle away from her. You were everything to me. I would have done anything for you." Naomi's words grieved her all the more, so she tightened her grip on Jeff's pillow and began to weep even louder, but her weeping was short-lived. Suddenly, Naomi heard the sound of Jeff's truck, and a few seconds later, she heard the beeping sounds of Jeff's truck alarm. With no time to spare, Naomi quickly placed Jeff's pillow in its rightful place, turned her body away from his side of the bed and pretended to be asleep. A few seconds later, he entered the bedroom.

Jeff was a handsome man, standing at six feet two and weighing a little over two hundred pounds. He had caramel colored skin, chestnut brown eyes, and what most referred to as a baby's face. Jeff's hair was cut into a semi-wavy, but short fade and his full, pink lips made him look like a model. His somewhat muscular body looked like a chiseled action figure. On the exterior, he was beautiful to look at, but his inner-man was hideous.

As Jeff removed his leather jacket, he could tell that his wife was not asleep. After all, Naomi was a snorer and she was not snoring. Jeff removed his pants and climbed into the bed next to his wife. He knew the routine. Normally, Naomi would pretend to wake up as he slipped into the bed and then, she'd ask him a lot of questions about where he'd been and whether or not he was having an affair. This time however, Naomi didn't follow her normal routine. Instead, she continued to face the window, all the while pretending to be asleep. Uncomfortable, Jeff flipped his pillow over and that's when he noticed how wet it was. It was soaked with Naomi's tears and it was obvious that she'd just finished crying into the pillow. Irritated, Jeff threw the pillow to the floor. He then climbed out of the bed, stormed into the living room and tried to sleep on the couch.

Don't feel sorry for Naomi just yet. Naomi hadn't been an angel herself. Before Jeff met her, he was married to a woman named Brianna. Brianna also had two children with Jeff and she was married to him for four years before he left her to be with his then mistress, Naomi. As a matter of fact, Naomi's oldest son, Melvin, was conceived four months before Jeff left his first wife. After Jeff's divorce was finalized, he married Naomi and the couple went on to have another son who they named Damien. The couple was now in their fifth year of marriage and it was obvious that Jeff was now doing to Naomi what he'd done to his first wife, Brianna. He was having an affair and Naomi knew who the other woman was. She was Naomi's ex-best friend, Carla. Their friendship ended when Naomi found raunchy pictures of Carla in Jeff's phone and of course, Jeff denied having an affair with Carla. He said that Carla had obviously gotten his number from Naomi somehow and she'd started texting him half-naked pictures of herself the same day that Naomi had seen the photos.

Naomi wanted to rush to the living room and confront her husband, but she knew that if she did, he'd only leave again. She needed to choose her battles wisely and she'd grown tired of Jeff's attitude towards her and their children. Naomi remained in the bed until the alarm went off. Once it did, she woke her sons up, dressed them for school, fed them breakfast and then, woke Jeff up so he could take them to school. This was the daily routine for the Spencer household. Everyday, Naomi would get the children ready for school , but Jeff would take them there. Naomi worked from eight to five each day, but her job was thirty minutes outside of Los Angeles, whereas, the kids' school was fifteen minutes in the opposite direction. As Jeff put on his shoes, he noticed his wife's odd behavior. She wasn't argumentative and it was obvious that she'd been thinking a lot. She wasn't wearing her normal professional attire. Instead, she was wearing a jogging suit and tennis shoes. Her long, black hair was pulled back into a pony tail and she wasn't wearing any makeup. It was obvious that she had a plan and Jeff wanted to know what that plan was, but he knew that the children couldn't be late for school. "Where are you going?" he asked, staring at his wife, but Naomi didn't answer his question. "The children will be late for school," she said. After staring at his wife for another minute,

Jeff grabbed his keys and went out the door behind his children. He didn't know what Naomi was up to, but he knew that when he returned, his wife would normally be headed to work.

The sound of Jeff's cellphone pierced the silence. It was his best friend and mentor, Harvey. Harvey was an educated man with a P.h.D. in Clinical Psychology and a Masters Degree in Business Administration. He was also an entrepreneur and an author of twelve books, all part of a series designed to teach men about the psyche of women. A handsome man himself, Harvey was seven years older than Jeff, but he was in no way a settled man. Harvey had what Jeff referred to as the ultimate bachelor pad: a four bedroom, two story home, spanning over 45,000 square feet. The house had an indoor pool, Jacuzzi, gym and private theater. Each of the bedrooms in the house was professionally decorated with a romantic theme.  Even though Harvey himself was a playboy, he often advised Jeff to be faithful to his wife.  Harvey would often say that as a Christian man, he respected marriage.  He would call Jeff once every few months to check in with him and make sure he was still on the path to success.  Harvey was a man obsessed with fame, glory, money and women.  He also prided himself as a Christian man, often incorporating spiritual advice with practical advice.  Even though Harvey said that he respected marriage, he would always brag about his rendezvouses with women to Jeff.  He'd also introduced Jeff to a few women in the past, but he'd always advised Jeff to not get serious about any of those women.  "Know the difference between a wife and a toy," Harvey would often tell Jeff.  "You have a wife.  Every other woman is a toy until you're tired of playing with her."

Jeff was surprised to see Harvey calling him so early in the morning.

"Hey man; what's up?"

"Nothing. Just calling to see how everything was going and to tell you some surprising news."

"Awe, man. With you, there are no surprises. How can I be like you?"

"Please. I need to be asking you the same thing. You're the one with the beautiful wife and perfect children. I'm trying to be like you."

"Yeah, yeah... but what's up?"

"Well, I know I haven't talked with you in a few months, and that's because I've been busy. As it turns out, I'm a father now."

"What?!"

"Yep. I have a nine month old son by the name of Henry, and check this... I have custody of him."

"Wait... How'd that happen? Before you

answer that, I know how it happened,
but who's the mother and why in the
world would she give her child to you?
Please tell me it isn't crazy Diana."
*Harvey laughs.*

"No, it's not *crazy* Diana. Ironically
enough, her name is also Dianna, but it's
spelled slightly different. Anyhow, I met
her about eighteen months ago and we
had a one night stand. I didn't know
until about nine months ago that she had
birthed a baby, and of course, I didn't
believe the child was mine. After all,
we'd slept together once and she'd never
called and told me that she was
pregnant. She simply called me from the
hospital because she wanted to give the
boy up for adoption. I came to the
hospital and they performed a paternity
test, and a few days later, I got a call
saying that the test indicated that the
boy was mine. I didn't know what to do.

I thought the test was rigged or something, so I had the child tested again, and the results came out the same. He's my boy. I couldn't let my own flesh and blood be given up for adoption, so I took custody of him. I didn't tell you because, at first, I wasn't sure if I was going to keep him. I thought I could get one of my sisters to raise him, but that didn't happen. I kept to myself for these last nine months, trying to get to know my son better, and now, I can honestly say I'm a proud father."

"That's awesome. I'm happy for you. Congratulations."

"Why, thank you. And he's an awesome kid. Seriously. Can you believe he's already walking at nine months old? He's definitely changed my life."

"Seriously, man; I'm happy for you. I can't wait to meet the little ladies' man."

"Yeah, I can't wait for you to meet him

either.  How's Melvin and Damien?"

"They're good.  I'm taking them to school right now.  It's their mother who's crazy."

"Uh oh.  What's wrong now?"

"You know women.  I made a joke about her hair last night and she took it personal.  I didn't feel like fighting, so I left."

"Jeff, don't tell me you stayed out all night again"

"I had to.  I didn't want to deal with Naomi's attitude, plus, you know... I kinda, sorta had plans myself."

"Man, seriously... Not Carla again.  You need to stop messing with that crazy chic.  I'm telling you she's more obsessed with your wife than she is with you.  I think the girl's gay or something.  Diana was crazy, but Carla is a certifiable nutcase.  I'd write that girl a prescription without her ever having to visit my office."

"Maybe so. I can't say too much right now, but man, oh man... Crazy or not, she got that magic touch... You know what I mean."

"Yeah, I know what you mean, but you need to stop for real. You're a married man and you have a good wife. Don't throw that away for some crazy woman who's obviously got a thing for your wife. Remember, separate the toys from the wife."

"I guess. Now, of course, Naomi's upset and I don't know what she's up to. She's been acting really strange, so I'm about to drop the kids off at school, and hopefully, I'll catch her before she leaves for work."

"There are a lot of men out there who'd kill to get what you got, Jeff. Hold on. My secretary's calling me. Let me give you a call back."

"Alright, man.  Congratulations again."

While driving five year old Melvin and four
year old Damien to school, Jeff found himself
obsessively thinking about his wife's
abnormal behavior.   He kept looking in the
rear view mirror to see if his sons
understood the conversation he'd just had
with Harvey.   "Where is your Mom going?"
he asked Melvin, but Melvin didn't answer.
Instead, he shrugged his shoulders and
continued to look out the window.  He was
angry with his dad for how he'd been
treating his mother, but little Damien
couldn't resist answering his father.  "I think
Mom is going to move in with Grandma
because she put some suitcases in her car
last night and I heard Grandma telling her to
come back home."  Melvin was agitated with
his little brother, so he shoved little Damien's
car seat and told his brother that he needed
to shut up sometimes.  Jeff, on the other

hand, became agitated, frustrated and scared. On one hand, he wanted to divorce his wife to be with Carla, but on the other hand, he was comfortable with Naomi.  After all, Naomi was the one who'd helped a once unemployed Jeff get hired as a sales representative for Advert-Eyes Marketing, one of the top sales and marketing companies in California.   Advert-Eyes was owned by Naomi's uncle, Dr. Richard Preston... a renowned Ophthalmologist who'd gathered a lot of success by creating and marketing his own custom brand of contact lenses.

Jeff dropped the children off at school and rushed back towards his house.  He called Naomi's cell phone while driving, but she did not answer his call.  His heart raced as he sped through traffic, eager to see what his wife was planning.  When he finally pulled into the garage, he was surprised and scared by what he saw. Naomi's car was still in the garage, and it was full of clothes, suitcases and toys. Jeff purposely pulled his truck in behind Naomi's car to ensure that she wouldn't be able to back out, but this meant the garage door could not close. As he exited his truck, he saw Naomi heading towards her car with another box. Her car was packed and it was obvious that the box would not fit in the car, but Naomi was determined to make it fit.

"What are you doing?"

"What does it look like I'm doing, Jeff? I'm leaving you."

"You better not have any of my stuff packed up in here!"

"Don't worry. I only have my clothes and the rest of my stuff, plus, the boys' clothes and a few of their toys. I don't want anything of yours."

"You're not taking the kids. You can leave, but they're staying here."

"Oh really?  Who's going to stop me?"

"What do you mean who's going to stop you?  I am!  Like I said, Naomi, you can leave, but you've got to leave the kids here."

"Okay.  Help me unpack their stuff."

Jeff was surprised that Naomi had given up so easily.  Was she really going to let him keep the kids?  Honestly, he didn't want to be burdened down with the kids and Naomi knew this.

"So, you're just going to walk away from your kids like that?  Your own flesh and blood?"

"Yep.  You're their father, so they're in good hands.  Anyhow, Momma has a two bedroom house.  There is no room there for the boys anyway, so you're probably doing me a favor.  We'll work out the visitation at the lawyer's office."

"Lawyer?  What do we need a lawyer

for?  Do you want a divorce, Naomi?"

"Let's see what options I have... Stay married to you and just deal with the fact that you're a terrible husband, a cheater and a lousy father or divorce you and get my sanity back.  Which one do you think I'm gonna pick?"

"I see what you're doing.  You think I'm gonna beg you to stay with me and everything will start going your way. The next thing you know I'll be wearing an apron and getting manicures.  No thank you.  You can leave.  Just send me the divorce papers and I'll sign them."

"Okay."

"Okay?"

"Yes.  I said okay.  What else do you want me to say?"

"I'm not keeping the kids.  You gotta take them with you if you're leaving."

"What?  Why?  You said you wanted to keep them."

"Nope. I changed my mind. Let me go find me a lawyer too."

At that, Jeff stormed into the house thinking that Naomi would follow him, but she didn't. A few minutes later, Jeff went to see if Naomi was still in the garage, but she wasn't. To his surprise, his truck had been moved by Naomi and parked into his normal parking space and she'd left. Jeff had forgotten that Naomi had a key to his truck. He rushed back into the house to call Naomi's cell phone, but when he did, he heard the sound of her phone ringing. He followed the sound to their bedroom where Naomi had left the phone on their bed. At first, he thought Naomi had accidentally left the phone there because of her rush to leave, but those thoughts were dispelled once he began to go through her phone. He checked her call log and noticed that his mistress, Carla, had called Naomi three times. The entire call log had been erased and the only number left in the call log and text messages was Carla's number. She'd called her the previous night and she'd called her twice that morning.

Jeff's heart raced as he continued to navigate through his wife's phone. He checked her text messages, and to his horror, he saw the dialogue his wife and mistress had been engaged in. It had started off with a message from Carla to Naomi, and the message read, "Guess where your husband is?" After that message, Carla had sent a picture of a sleeping and naked Jeff to his horrified wife. The two had engaged in a war of words, but that war had ended when Carla sent Naomi a picture of a positive pregnancy test with a message that read, "Yes, it belongs to Jeff. I guess it's your time to exit the picture."

Naomi responded by sending Carla a message that read, "I don't know what I've done to you to make you hate me. I was truly your friend, but I do understand that I'm just getting back everything I took his first wife through. I still love you, Carla, and I'm not angry with you anymore. I forgive you and I pray that your relationship with Jeff is a happy one. I won't fight you for him anymore. He's yours. I've cried my last tears over him. Now, I'm handing that torch to you."

Jeff's heart was racing. It was at that moment that he realized he wasn't ready to divorce Naomi. At the same time, Carla hadn't mentioned to him that she was pregnant and after seeing her texts to his wife, Jeff was sure of one thing: He did not want to continue his relationship with Carla.

Jeff jumped into his Jeep Rover and sped towards his mother-in-law's house. He called Ms. Bloomfield (his mother-in-law), but she didn't answer the phone. He then called Carla to confront her about the text messages and the pregnancy test.

"I was expecting your call. I guess you talked to Naomi."

"Why did you text her last night, Carla? I thought we agreed that I would leave Naomi when the time was right."

"The time was right for me, Jeff. I'm pregnant."

"Yeah... about that... Why didn't you tell me that you were pregnant? Or is this some kind of sick game?"

"No, I'm really pregnant. The doctor said I'm about four months into the pregnancy... maybe five months. I was going to tell you, but..."

"But what? You couldn't resist sending that text to Naomi... and how do I know the baby's mine anyway?!"

"You'll know when the baby is born. You are more than welcome to get a DNA test."

"I don't care if it is or if it isn't. It's over

between you and me.  What you did was messed up.  I'm gonna try to go and get my wife back, and when I do, don't call us anymore.  It's over!"

*Carla began to laugh.*

"Oh, you don't know Naomi very well, do you?  She's not going to take you back. She's got too much pride.  I'm surprised she stayed with you this long."

"What are you talking about, Carla?"

"Naomi has her issues, but she walks away from any man who cheats on her. She's stronger than she looks... believe me.  I'm not sure if she told you, but she was pregnant by a guy named Lonnie one time.  She found out that Lonnie had been cheating on her, so she left without ever looking back.  She miscarried their son, and to this day, he still asks about her."

"You sound like her greatest fan.  How do you know that he still asks about her?"

"I just do."

"But how do you know?"

"Like I said, I just do.  Let's drop it, okay?
We need to be talking about our growing
family... not your soon-to-be ex-wife."

With that, Jeff hung up the phone and
continued driving towards his mother-in-
law's house.  A few minutes before he
reached his destination, Jeff received a text
message from Harvey that read, "Let God
handle it."  Jeff tossed his phone back onto
the passenger's seat and continued on his
way.

*"For there is nothing hid, which shall not be manifested; neither was any thing kept secret, but that it should come abroad."*

(Mark 4:22/ KJV)

## Chapter 2

## All Played Out

When Jeff finally arrived at his mother-in-law's house, he saw Naomi's car parked out front alongside a car he didn't recognize. It was a red sports type vehicle with a convertible top, but there was no tag on the back of the vehicle. The only identifiable clue as to who the car belonged to was a tag on the front of the vehicle that read, "DuNa Rules". Curious, Jeff exited his truck and made his way towards the front door of the house. As he walked past the red convertible, he slowed his pace and peered into the car. The car was obviously new and the white leather interior was flawless. Jeff suddenly remembered Naomi's cousin, Donna. He thought to himself that the car was likely Donna's vehicle and she'd just found a creative way to spell her name.

The front door of the house was open; the only door that was bolted shut was the storm door. Jeff knocked on the door, and then, placed his face close to it so he could see inside the house. He used his hands to block the sunlight as he peered into his mother-in-law's home. In the distance, he could see what appeared to be a toddler, no more than nine or ten months old. The rambunctious little boy was sitting on the floor in the dining room. He appeared to be laughing at someone, but whomever he was being entertained by was not visible because the toddler was sitting near the entry door to the dining room. The toddler's almost fiery-red, curly hair complemented his beautiful, medium brown skin. His chestnut brown

eyes looked a lot like Jeff's eyes and his wide
smile reminded Jeff of his own smile. Who
was this child? Just as Jeff was about to
knock again, he felt a tap on his shoulder.
Chills ran down his spine as he turned
around to see a tall, rugged looking brother
staring back at him. "Duke, who is that?" A
voice could be heard coming from the left
side of the house, but the tall, muscular man
didn't answer. Instead, he continued to stare
at Jeff, waiting for him to explain himself.

Duke looked a lot like Jeff. He was a tall,
muscular brother standing at six feet, five
inches with medium brown skin and
chestnut brown eyes. Unlike Jeff, however,
Duke had deep set, almond-shaped eyes and
his eyebrows were somewhat thick. It was
obvious that the toddler Jeff had seen in the
house was the son of Duke or he was closely
related to him.
"Hi, my name is Jeff and I'm Naomi's

husband..." Before he could finish his sentence, Duke punched Jeff with so much force that he spun around before falling face forward to the ground. Jeff's mind raced as he tried to lift himself from the ground. Who was this guy and why had he hit him? Before Jeff could stand to his feet, the front door of the house flung open and three men rushed out to restrain the now enraged Duke. "You killed my wife, you dirty animal!" screamed Duke as the men tried to carry him into the house. "Let me loose, so I can finish this scumbag! Y'all seriously... let me loose! Let me loose!" Duke's voice became more and more distant as the men carried him into the house and into another room.

Jeff stumbled towards his truck, still somewhat dazed from the punch. He noticed blood on his shirt, so he lifted his hand and touched his mouth to see if it was bleeding. It was obvious that one of his teeth was loose and his mouth was full of blood. When Jeff arrived at his truck, he opened the door and sat in the driver's seat, but he did not close the door. Suddenly, he noticed the front door of the house opening, and to his surprise, he saw Naomi approaching the vehicle. Jeff wanted to look into her eyes to see if there was any hope for their marriage, but as she approached the vehicle, Naomi continued to look at the ground. It was almost like she was a different person. She was carrying a towel in one hand and in the other hand, she had an envelope.

"Here. Use this towel to clean yourself up," said Naomi. Jeff looked at his wife's extended hand for a few seconds before reaching for the towel.

"So, I'm guessing that the guy who punched me is your boyfriend."

"No, he was Robyn's husband."

"Robyn?"

"Yeah, remember I told you I had a sister who died last year... the sister you said you'd never met?"

"Yeah, I remember, but didn't you tell me her name was Michelle?"

"Michelle was her middle name. We called her by her middle name."

"But why did the guy say I killed his wife? I didn't even know Michelle."

"Yes, you did."

Naomi extended the envelope to her newly estranged husband.

"Open this."

"What is it?"

"Well, you know how you've been keeping secrets from me all of these years. I've kinda been keeping a secret from you too."

Confused, Jeff reached for the envelope, but as he opened the envelope, he could not take his eyes off his wife.  He was used to seeing Naomi with makeup on and she always wore her hair down, but with her hair pulled back in a pony tail, she suddenly began to look like a woman he once knew... a woman named Robyn.  It couldn't be "his" Robyn.  After all, Robyn was a woman Jeff had cheated with almost two years ago.  She was a married woman who'd just moved to Los Angeles from Dallas, Texas.  Robyn told Jeff that she and her husband moved to California after her husband won a settlement against a company he once worked for.  The company had wrongfully terminated her husband and had him arrested because more than three million dollars had been stolen from the company.  Her husband had been the only black man working for them and they assumed he was responsible for the theft, but they had no evidence to prove their suspicions.  Because the company's C.E.O. was convinced that her husband was guilty, he'd wrongfully terminated him and given a false statement to authorities, claiming that the computer where all of the wire transfers had been made belonged to him. In truth, the computer belonged to the C.E.O.'s own son, but he didn't want to believe that his son could be guilty of such a heinous crime. After all, the C.E.O. was rich and his son didn't want for anything. It made absolutely no sense to anyone that Mark (the son of the C.E.O.) could be guilty of embezzlement. Robyn's husband had been arrested and served two years in a federal prison before Mark finally confessed his crime to the authorities via a suicide note. Mark had attempted to take his life by shooting himself in the head, but the bullet had only grazed his head before Mark went unconscious. Mark's wife heard the gunshot, rushed to the room and tried to revive her unconscious husband. She'd also called the police, and when the officers arrived, they found Mark's suicide note. Once the new evidence came to light, Robyn's husband was released from prison and he successfully sued the company for eight point one million dollars.

Jeff pulled the pictures from the envelope and was horrified at what he saw. The sister Naomi had so lovingly referred to as Michelle was the woman he'd had an affair with. Her name was Robyn Michelle Raisman. He didn't know that Michelle was Naomi's little sister, Robyn; after all, Naomi had never introduced him to Robyn and she'd rarely spoken of her. It was as if she didn't exist. Robyn and Naomi had a rather contentious relationship, and because of this, the two hadn't spoken in six years. According to Naomi, Michelle (aka Robyn) had always gone after every man she'd ever been romantically involved with. After she'd been caught in bed with Naomi's ex-fiance some six years ago, Naomi had stopped speaking with her sister, vowing to never talk to her again.  Robyn was angry about her sister's estrangement from her life and she'd made it her life's goal to hurt Naomi all the more. When Robyn and her husband moved to Los Angeles, she hadn't told Naomi about her move.  Naomi heard about it from her mother.  What Naomi didn't know, however, was that Robyn was up to her old tricks. She'd seen pictures of Naomi and Jeff at their mother's house and that's why she'd married Duke.  Duke looked a lot like Jeff, but he was a little taller and much more handsome than Jeff.  Nevertheless, Robyn wasn't satisfied with Duke because she was determined to ruin her sister's life.  She was angry with Naomi for disassociating from her because Robyn mistakenly believed that regardless of the evils she'd done to her sister, Naomi was supposed to remain an active part of her life. She was especially angry that Naomi had nothing to do with her thirteen year old daughter, Krísi. After all, Krísi admired her aunt Naomi and would often ask about her.

Once Duke got his settlement, Robyn had insisted that they move to Los Angeles. She knew that Duke wanted to start his own marketing firm and gym and she'd convinced him that California was the best place for him to invest his money. After the couple moved to Los Angeles, Robyn had reached out to her sister, Naomi, in an attempt to reconcile their relationship, but Naomi would not return her calls. She knew that her sister had not changed and was still obsessed with ruining her life. Angry about her sister's rejection, Robyn, pretending to be interested in reconciling with her sister, had asked their mother about Naomi and found out that Jeff, Naomi's husband, was working for their Uncle Richard at Advert-Eyes. After discovering that Jeff worked for Advert-Eyes, Robyn went to the company a few nights just before the office closed and watched Jeff whenever he went to his car. One night, Robyn parked her car a few feet away from Jeff's car, lifted her hood and pretended that her car wouldn't start. She'd loosened the battery's cable and waited for an unsuspecting Jeff to make his way to his car. After Jeff saw Robyn with her hood up, he couldn't resist offering the shapely beauty with the bronze skin a ride home. After all, Jeff was no mechanic, but he was an adulterer. The two immediately began to engage in an adulterous affair... an affair that was only cut short after Robyn was killed in a car accident.

Jeff was numb as he looked through the pictures of the woman he'd once referred to as the most beautiful woman he'd ever seen.

"So, this is your sister?"

"Yep. And you are responsible for her death."

"How? I can't lie. I do know her. I did sleep with her when we were having problems about a year or two ago, but I haven't seen her in a long time. Honestly, I didn't know she was dead. I thought she'd just stopped returning my calls because the last text message I'd gotten from her said that her husband had seen her with me. How am I responsible for her death?"

"About nine or ten months ago, I had a miscarriage, remember?"

"Yes, I remember."

"Well, what I didn't tell you was why I miscarried our son. It wasn't just that I'd lost my sister. My mother finally told me that Robyn had died in a car accident after her husband, Duke, hired a private investigator to follow her. You see, Duke started suspecting that Robyn was having an affair when saw your number on her cell phone bill. He said your

number was on every page of the bill
and that's why he got suspicious. Robyn
had been leaving every night around
nine.... the same time you got off work.
He hired a private investigator and the
investigator confirmed that Robyn was
having an affair. He took a lot of pictures
of the two of you, but of course, I'm not
bringing them out right now because I'll
be using them in court. Anyhow, Robyn
had just given birth to her son a month
before the accident and she would leave
her infant at home with Duke, claiming
that she was going to the gym. On the
night of her death, Duke took their son
to a neighbor's house and went to the
hotel where the investigator said the
two of you often met up. You were
always a creature of habit, Jeff, and that's
why it was no surprise to me that you
had Robyn meet you in the same room
every time you met up.... room 712.

Duke sat out in his car and waited for you to leave the room, since according to the private investigator, you would always leave first, and then, Robyn would leave about twenty minutes later. When Robyn left the room, she saw her husband sitting on the hood of his car, waiting for her. I guess she panicked because she got into her car and sped away. Duke said he didn't chase her because he knew she had to come home. Anyhow, my guess is that Robyn was so scared that she didn't pay attention to where she was going, so according to the police report, she was speeding down the highway and somehow, lost control of the car. Her car went off the road and flipped at least five times before landing upside down. She was dead by the time paramedics arrived."

Jeff didn't know what to say. His entire body

was numb and it was in that moment that he realized that his life was about to change for the worse.

"Why didn't you tell me about her? Why would you stay with me after that? And I don't remember you going to her funeral."

"I loved you, Jeff, and at first, I blamed my sister. I didn't go to her funeral because I was mad at her. I was pregnant and I wasn't ready to end it all yet. When I lost our son, I still didn't feel strong enough to be without you. I begged my mother to not say anything to you about Robyn and that was easy considering the two of you didn't talk anyway. She convinced Duke to keep quiet until I was ready. I guess I'm ready now. I want a divorce, Jeff. Just tell me what you want and you can have it."

"Wow. I don't know what to say, Naomi. I'm hurt, scared, confused and I don't know what to do or say right now. I feel like anything I say is wrong because.... man, according to y'all, I'm responsible for Robyn's death. Wow. What do you say to something like that? I mean... I do love you, baby and I know I wasn't the best husband to you, but I do love you. Now, I don't think I'm ready to let go just yet. What about us? What about Melvin and Damien? We've got two beautiful children together."

"That's another thing I wanted to speak with you about. Duke's son, as it turns out, is not his son. My guess is that little Duke Jr. should have been named Jeff Jr."

"Wait-a-minute... I knew she'd gotten pregnant and she told me that she was pregnant by her husband... not me. I didn't get Robyn pregnant, but I did continue to see her when she was pregnant... that I can admit."

"Duke just got the results back from the

paternity test a few weeks ago. Little Duke is not his son. Honestly, I knew he was yours the minute I laid eyes on him. He looks just like Damien... they could actually go for twins if Damien was his age. I guess I was just in denial; after all, you do favor Duke Sr."

"No. I'm sorry. I can't let you blame me for the baby. Robyn and I always used condoms... always!"

"That's a lie and I can tell you how I know. Robyn is allergic to latex and she's allergic to polyurethane. Whenever Robyn would decide to have a sexual relationship with a man, she would always make that man go to a doctor and get tested for any and every sexually transmitted disease known to man. I can almost guarantee you that the minute Robyn decided to sleep with you, she sent you to her doctor to be tested."

With that, Jeff dropped his head. He knew that Robyn had sent him to her doctor to be tested. He didn't know, however, that Robyn was allergic to latex and polyurethane. She'd always told him that she couldn't have any more children because her tubes were tied. She also said that she didn't like condoms, so she preferred to have what she referred to as "intimate sex", or better yet, sex without a condom. Jeff had gotten tested at Robyn's request and the two had never used any contraceptives.

"Where do we go from here?" Jeff asked, dropping his head.

"We divorce," said Naomi. "I don't want anything from you, Jeff. I don't even want child support from you. I just want you to give me the divorce and I don't want you in our sons' lives. I want you to sign away your parental rights and leave me and my family alone."

"I'm not walking out of our sons' lives,

Naomi. I'm sorry. That's something I cannot do."

"You walked out of Brianna's life and you haven't had anything to do with Jessica or Jeff Jr. since the day you divorced their mother. You don't have much of anything to do with Melvin and Damien and you live in the same house with them. I get up everyday and get them ready for school; I cook for them, help them with their homework, go to the parent/ teacher meetings and I play with them everyday. The only thing you do is take them to school and boss them around. I bet you don't even know their favorite colors or their favorite songs."

"Naomi, a boy needs his father and I know I wasn't the best man to you, but I don't want to walk out of my children's lives. That's something I can't do."

"Okay. That's fair. You don't have to sign over your rights. I'll talk with my attorney to see how much child support I should be getting.  With the amount of money you make, we should live comfortably."

"Why are you doing this, Naomi?"

"Doing what?"

"I see what you're doing.  You're trying to scare me by talking about child support."

"No, I'm not.  I'm going to see my lawyer tomorrow; I already have an appointment and I want to know what to tell him when I walk through the doors."

After his conversation with Naomi ended, Jeff got in his truck and left.  His lip had swollen up by then and he was sure that his bottom tooth was about to fall out of his mouth.  He immediately picked up his phone and responded to Harvey's text.  "It looks like we're brothers after all.  I just found out that I may possibly be the father of a child by a woman who turns out to be one of Naomi's sisters. Call you when I clear my head." Harvey tried to call Jeff, but he wouldn't answer his phone. One hour after Jeff left his mother-in-law's house, he called Naomi. "I'll sign over the rights to the boys on one condition. Don't bring up our personal issues in court. Don't bring up Carla and don't bring up Robyn. I feel bad about what I did and I don't want to relive those stories anymore. I want this to be over with and quick." Naomi agreed to Jeff's terms and six months later, the two came to court for their final hearing. Jeff signed over his parental rights to Melvin and Damien, and after his divorce was finalized, he married Carla.

# Chapter 3

## Unveiled Deception

A year had past since Jeff and Naomi's divorce and Jeff was now separated from Carla. As it turns out, Jeff simply could not be faithful, so he had an affair with one of Carla's friends. That friend gave Jeff gonorrhea, and of course, he gave the disease to his wife. To make matters worse, he lost his job with Advert-Eyes after it was discovered that he had an affair with a new intern he was assigned to train. Jeff's life was spiraling out of control and he couldn't stop thinking about what he believed to be the highest point of his life... when he was married to Naomi. When he was married to

Naomi, Jeff had a job making almost six figures; he had two beautiful children, a home that most people dreamed of and a wife who was effortlessly beautiful.

It was around nine o'clock on a Saturday night when Jeff found himself obsessively thinking about Brianna and Naomi. Brianna, in Jeff's opinion, had been the best wife he'd ever had. She loved him, remained faithful to him and she'd worked hard to make their marriage work, even though the couple had struggled financially the entire length of their marriage because Jeff was working in a pizza shop while Brianna was going to school. Naomi, on the other hand, was a decent wife, but Jeff was obsessed with her beauty, her seductive tendencies and her overflowing confidence. Additionally, Jeff knew that if he was with Naomi, he'd be financially stable because Naomi's family was full of successful men and women who either built careers

working for other companies or they had
started and run their own.

Jeff was in his new apartment browsing
Facebook when he began to think about his
exes.  He looked for Brianna on Facebook,
but she didn't have a profile.  That was just
like Brianna.  She was a very private woman
who saw social media as nothing more than a
platform for socially rejected people who
longed for acceptance.  After searching for
Brianna's profile, Jeff decided to search for
Naomi's profile on Facebook, but at first, he
couldn't find her.  He typed in her maiden
name and her profile didn't show up.  He
typed in "Spencer", which, of course, was his
surname, but that name didn't show up
either.  Was she on Facebook, or worse, had
she married someone else?  Jeff began typing
in some of Naomi's family members' names,
and it wasn't long before he came across a
comment left by Naomi under her brother,

Ruben's photos. Jeff was horrified at what he saw. Naomi was listed as Naomi Raisman. Wait a minute. Raisman was Robyn's married name, plus, Naomi's profile picture was a photo of her kissing a sleeping man and that man looked a lot like Duke. Did Naomi marry her deceased sister's husband? Jeff could feel his muscles tensing up as his heart began to race. He clicked on Naomi's photo, but he couldn't see the face of the man clearly. He simply looked like Duke. Maybe Naomi had married one of Duke's relatives. Either way, the thought alone of Naomi being with someone else made Jeff sick to his stomach. He began to go through Naomi's photos and his worst nightmare was confirmed. Naomi was married to Duke, and even worse, there were many pictures of Duke playing with Melvin and Damien. In one photo, Duke was giving Damien a piggy back ride, and in another photo, he was arm wrestling with Melvin. Jeff's anger could barely be contained, but he tried to maintain his composure while browsing through the photos. The photo that hurt and shocked him most was the picture of Duke kissing a very pregnant Naomi's belly. Jeff stared at the photo in horror and just when he thought things couldn't get any worse, the next photo made him shiver with anger. It was a professional family photo and on the photo, Duke was seated and holding what appeared to be a newborn baby girl. Naomi was standing next to Duke with one hand on Duke's shoulder, and the other hand on Melvin's shoulder. Damien stood on the other side of Duke and he was looking at Duke while wearing a huge but not forced smile on his face. Lastly, in front of Duke stood Robyn's son, Duke Jr. and Jeff could tell that little Duke was definitely his son. He looked a lot like Melvin, but he had Damien's almost perfect eyebrows. How long had Naomi been seeing Duke and was her relationship with Duke the reason she'd insisted that Jeff turn over his parental rights? Jeff began to read the comments under the family photo and he found himself offended by the number of family members who'd commented in support of the awkward family. Many of those same family members hadn't approved of Jeff. As a matter of fact, many of them hadn't attended Jeff and Naomi's wedding, nor had they ever visited the couple.

As Jeff continued to read the comments, one of them caught him off guard. The comment was made by a woman who looked a lot like Robyn, but that was impossible; after all, Robyn was supposed to be dead. The woman called herself Robyn's Gemela. What type of sick scheme had Robyn and Naomi cooked up? Jeff was enraged, confused and growing more and more anxious by the minute. He clicked on Robyn's Gemela profile and started to browse through her photos. "That's Robyn, alright!" he said aloud as he scrolled through the hundreds of photos posted on her profile. The one photo that scared him the most was the photo of Robyn holding Duke Jr. in the air. In the photo, Duke Sr. was standing next to her and Naomi was behind Duke with her arms wrapped around him. The last photo only added to the mystery. In the photo, Duke and Naomi were seated in the red convertible that Jeff had seen the day he went to his ex-mother-in-law's house. It was all beginning to make sense. The words "DuNa" on the tag obviously meant Duke and Naomi. Jeff had originally thought the car belonged to Naomi's cousin, Donna, and she'd just found a creative way to spell her name. Jeff was desperate for answers, so he navigated back to Naomi's profile and sent her a message that read:

*Hey there. I see you've moved on with*

*your life. You lied to me, Naomi. I was an
awful husband; I understand that, but
this sick, twisted game that you and
Robyn played is far worse than anything
my dirty mind could have cooked up. So,
I'm guessing that Duke was your guy all
along and maybe Robyn test drove him
for you? Did I get that right? Don't
bother telling me that Robyn is dead. I
saw her page as well and I'm guessing
she's remarried too. Anyhow, I won't take
too much of your time, but I wanted to let
you know that I want my rights to ALL of
my children reinstated (that includes
Duke, Jr.) and I will be hiring a lawyer
first thing tomorrow. You could have just
been honest with me. This level of
deception goes beyond ghetto. This is the
kind of horror story that only Stephen
King could cook up. Oh, and don't bother
trying to scare or intimidate me. I gave
up my rights because I had a lot to lose,*

*but now, you're dealing with a man who has nothing to lose, but everything to gain.*

Jeff opened another browser window and began to search for lawyers in his area. He was about five minutes into his search when he decided to take a break and go back through what he believed to be Robyn's profile. As he scrolled through her photos, he found himself being pulled in by her beauty once again. She was, without a shadow of a doubt, the most beautiful woman that Jeff had ever laid eyes on. For a moment, he found himself so caught up in Robyn's beauty that he almost forgot why he was on her profile page. "You're one sexy devil," he whispered as he navigated through Robyn's page. He also saw pictures of Robyn cuddling up with her daughter, Krísi. Jeff had never met Krísi, but he'd seen a few photos of her, so he recognized her immediately. After all,

Krísi was uniquely beautiful, just like her
mother.  Suddenly, the message light lit up
indicating that he'd received an inbox
message.   It was from Naomi and he couldn't
wait to open the message to see what she
had to say.

*Dear Jeff,*

*I hope all is well in your life.  Carla*
*reached out to me several times (Lord,*
*help her) and she told me about your*
*recent separation.  Let me first say that I*
*am truly sorry to hear about your*
*impending divorce.  I honestly thought*
*that you and Carla were perfect for each*
*other and I don't mean that in a bad way.*
*I see she's still obsessed with my life.*
*Honestly, she's been writing me every*
*other month trying to apologize for her*
*affair with you.  For whatever reason, she*
*also felt the need to tell me about her*
*failing marriage to you, but I've never*
*answered her because I didn't want to*

*open that door. Secondly, you signed over*
*your rights to the boys. That was your*
*decision, not mine. I still have the text*
*message you sent me and I warned my*
*lawyer that you may change your mind*
*after you found out that Duke and I are*
*an item. So, we are already ready to*
*counter anything you say or do. Was I*
*seeing Duke while I was married to you?*
*No. When I found out that you were*
*responsible for Robyn's death, Duke and I*
*grew close, but we weren't an item.*
*Remember, I didn't tell you that Robyn*
*was my sister even after I found out about*
*the two of you because I first blamed*
*Robyn for her own death. Nevertheless, I*
*felt bad for Duke and I begged him time*
*and time again not to confront you about*
*his wife; so yes, I did grow close to him*
*while we were married, but we were only*
*friends. It wasn't until after we broke up*
*that Duke and I got involved. Lastly, the*

*page you mentioned (Robyn's Gesola) is
not Robyn's page. Robyn is dead and I
have the obituary to prove it. Gesola
means "twin" in Spanish or did you forget
that I told you I have five brothers and
three sisters, and two of my sisters were
twins? You never stopped to listen to me
nor did you try to get to know my family,
so I didn't press it. That page was created
by Ravyn, who, by the way, is Robyn's
twin. You've never been too interested in
hearing about my family and that's why
you obviously didn't pay attention when I
told you about them. Ravyn and Robyn
were close, so when Robyn stopped
speaking to me, Ravyn stopped speaking
to me. Ravyn has been living in Mexico
for the last seven years and she's never
been very family oriented. Robyn is dead;
Ravyn is her twin, and Ravyn has custody
of Robyn's daughter, Krísi. I have custody
of the son Robyn had with you. Anyhow, I*

*hope you enjoyed browsing through our pages, because by the time you read this message, your account will be blocked. You are more than welcome to open another account to stalk our pages, but please beware that anything you say or do will be used against you (not me) in a court of law. See you in court, and by the way, Duke and the kids said, "Hi!"*

After reading the note, Jeff's caramel colored skin had turned fiery red. He was angry and embarrassed and his pride had taken an almost fatal hit. He did remember Naomi mentioning having twins in her family, but he didn't know that Robyn had a twin. After all, Robyn had never mentioned her twin sister to him. He did know that Robyn was secretive because it took her more than a month to tell him about her daughter, Krísi. Why was Carla still reaching out to Naomi? It was clear that Naomi wasn't interested in her. Jeff was livid. His sons were being raised by a man who should have been their uncle and one of his sons (Duke, Jr.) was being raised by the woman who should have been his biological mother. The whole situation was messed up and Jeff was ashamed to be a part of it. He decided not to go up against Naomi in court because he didn't want the circus he called life to be put on display for others to see. Jeff believed that his background as a salesmen pretty much guaranteed him a successful future with another sales and marketing company, so he wanted to keep his life as drama free as possible.

Curious about Carla's decision to reach out to Naomi, Jeff decided to visit Carla's Facebook page and he was shocked to see that her most recent post had been posted two minutes ago. Carla had posted an old photo of her and Naomi, along with a comment that

read, "You were there for me when no one else was.  I need you now more than ever."
Why was Carla so obsessed with Naomi?
What did she expect to achieve by that post?

*"For by means of a whorish woman a man is brought to a piece of bread: and the adulteress will hunt for the precious life."* (Proverbs 6:26/ KJV)

## Chapter 4

# When the Adulteress Takes Off Her Mask

As the years passed, Jeff found himself in one relationship after the other, never taking the time to settle down and find himself. With each relationship, he grew more and more promiscuous, and with each failed relationship, he found himself obsessing over Brianna and Naomi all the more. Brianna moved on and married the son of a local and prominent pastor. The couple went on to have three more children together. Naomi and Duke remained married for seven and a half years. Their marriage ended because both Naomi and Duke repeatedly committed adultery against one another. Duke went on to remarry and he got custody of his daughter with Naomi. Carla and Jeff divorced and after their divorce, Carla seemed to disappear off the radar.

It was twelve years later and Jeff was in town for a fireman's convention. He'd been working for the fire department in Tempe, Arizona for the last ten years. He'd relocated to Arizona after his problems with women had gotten him arrested three times, not to mention, there were several women after him for back child support. It was the first day of the convention and after it ended for the day, Jeff decided to go by the local gym. He was still health conscious, even though his once smooth, peanut butter-like skin was now covered with razor bumps and frown lines. Nevertheless, he was still considered a very handsome man... for his age.

While at the gym, Jeff saw a somewhat muscular young man walk through the door. There was no denying it... it was Jeff's son, Melvin. He walked right past his father and started towards the weights. Jeff watched from afar as his son began to warm up for his workout. He'd grown up to be a handsome young man and Jeff couldn't resist reintroducing himself to his son.

Jeff was nervous as he made his way towards Melvin, but before he could reach him, he heard a familiar voice calling from behind him. It was Naomi's voice. She'd dropped Melvin off at the gym and it was obvious that he'd forgotten something. "You'd forget your head if it wasn't screwed on," she joked as she made her way past Jeff and towards her son. Melvin laughed and reached for his workout gloves before thanking his mother. A few seconds later, Naomi turned around to head out the door and she found herself face-to-face with her ex-husband.

"Jeff?"

"In the flesh. How are you, Naomi?"

"What are you doing here? I thought you'd moved to Arizona."

"I did. I'm just in town for a few days. You're still looking good."

"Look, Jeff... Please don't bother Melvin. He's had it hard these last few years and I don't want you to burden him with..."

"Oh, so I'm a burden? I'm his father, Naomi. I may have been a burden to you, but I won't be a burden to my son."

"Jeff, you and I both know that you're unstable. You'll come into his life, get his hopes up and then, you'll up and disappear. I've had to nurse the wounds you left behind before and I don't want to have to do it again."

"The wounds I left behind? You're the one who insisted that I sign over my rights to my sons just so you could pursue some sick, twisted relationship with your dead sister's husband."

"Look, Jeff. That's over and done with. I don't want to dig up the past, nor do I want the past visiting me or my children."

Naomi hadn't aged much. As a matter of fact, she almost looked the same way as she'd looked when she was married to Jeff. The only difference was that she was beginning to look a lot like her mother, but in a good way. Her hair was no longer long. She'd cut it in a short hairdo that framed her beautiful, brown face with perfection. Naomi was, without a shadow of a doubt, a beautiful woman, but she was also a woman who could not be trusted.

Melvin noticed his mother talking with Jeff, but at first, he didn't know it was his father because he couldn't see his face too clearly.

However, he knew that his mother's body language and her failed attempt at a hushed tone meant that whoever the guy was, she didn't like him.

Melvin approached his parents, ready to defend his mother if he had to. "Is there a problem?" he asked. At that moment, Melvin's eyes grew big when Jeff turned to look at him. Melvin remembered his father, but his memories of him weren't good. As a matter of fact, Melvin had gone through counseling because of the hatred he'd once harbored towards his estranged father... a hatred that affected his schoolwork and behavior. Melvin was speechless. He couldn't find the words to say to the man who'd walked out of his life more than a decade ago. He couldn't find the right words to say to the man who'd hurt his mother time and time again, so he walked away with Jeff in pursuit of him.

"Stop, Melvin. Please let me talk with

you."

"For what?  You signed over your rights to talk to me."

"Melvin, let me explain everything to you.  This had everything to do with your mother... not me.  I want you to know the truth.  Stop walking and listen to me!"

Jeff's voice was loud and it was obvious that he was not only angry, but he was determined to turn Melvin against his mother.  Melvin stormed out of the gym and Naomi walked out of the gym in pursuit of her son, all the while, telling Jeff to leave them alone.  Jeff pursued the duo outside and just when Naomi was about to push him away from her son, Melvin suddenly turned around, pulled his mother's body behind him and stepped up to his father's face.

"What do you have to tell me?!  Huh?!  You were never a father, even when we lived with you!  You spent your entire existence chasing behind women and we all had to stand in line while you selfishly put everything else in front of us!  So, what do you want to tell me about my mother... huh?  That she asked, or better yet, coerced you into signing over your rights to us?!  Don't you think I know the story?!  My mom doesn't lie to any of us!  Do you think I'm angry with her for that?!  Well, I'm not!  That was the best decision she's ever made for Damien and I!  The worst decision she's ever made was choosing a sloppy, irresponsible boy like yourself to breed with!  I watched my mother cry everyday because of you and I couldn't wait to grow up and give you a grown man's spanking, and now that I'm old enough to give it to you, do you really want to be pursuing me and disrespecting my mother?!  She asked you to sign over your rights.... so what?!  Let's be honest here... You did it because you didn't want to have to pay child

support!  She didn't put a gun to your head;
she threatened to go after you for child
support and that was all it took!  You didn't
want her to take your precious quarters
away, so you signed those documents and
didn't look back.  You made a choice!  Now
stop being a grown baby and man up to your
own mistakes!  It's time for you to take
accountability for your own choices and stop
blaming everybody else!  I have a son now
and no woman in this world could make me
give up my rights to him!  So, thank you for
showing me what it's like to grow up without
a father.  Because of you, I will never walk
out of my son's life!  I'm more of a man than
you'll ever be!  Better yet, thank you for not
being in my life because I don't want to be
anything like you, Jeff!  Do yourself a favor!
Stay out of my life and you sure as hell better
stay out of my mom's face!  Because the next
time you raise your voice at the woman, who,
by the way, didn't sign over her rights to us,

I'm gonna give you that past due grown man's spanking that you're asking for."

With that, Melvin walked off angrily, leaving his humbled father and mother behind. Jeff stood on the sidewalk and watched as the small crowd of people who'd gathered to hear Melvin lashing out at his father began to disperse. One of the women in the crowd made eye contact with Jeff long enough for him to see her shaking her head in disgust as she grabbed her son's hand and walked in the opposite direction. Another man pursued Melvin, and Jeff could see in the distance that the man not only hugged Melvin, but he handed him his business card. When Jeff turned to look at Naomi, he saw something in her he'd never seen before. He saw pure evil. She didn't want to see her son hurting again, and even though she knew she was partly to blame for his pain, in that moment, she blamed Jeff. She wanted Jeff to hurt the same way she was hurting, so she walked up to him and calmly said the words that would forever change his life.

"The child I miscarried was not yours, so you don't have to beat yourself up anymore."

Naomi dropped her head and stepped closer to Jeff. She lowered her voice and began to unleash a truth on him that would rip through his soul.

"As a matter of fact, I didn't miscarry the child at all. I went to Ravyn's house in Mexico and gave birth to a healthy baby boy who I named Henry."

*Jeff covered his mouth.*

"Henry?"

"Yes, Henry."

"As in my best friend, Harvey's son, Henry?"

"Yes. As in your best friend who wasn't really your best friend after all. Henry is my son with Harvey."

"Harvey... as in my best friend?"

"Yes, Jeff. Are you deaf, Jeff? I had an affair with Harvey. You'd been cheating on me with anything that moved and I just wanted someone to talk to about your ways. I turned to Harvey hoping that he could help to steer you in the right direction, but instead, Harvey comforted me. He started helping me to see how valuable I was as a woman. You see, I learned that by making you my everything, I'd lost my own identity. At first, Harvey was just mentoring me, but it wasn't long before we'd crossed the point of no return. I went to his house one night crying about you and Carla, and of course, Harvey was enraged because, as he put it, you were a man who had everything, but you were too stupid and blind to see it. He held me and one thing led to another. We both felt bad about what we'd done, but it was too late. You can't take sex back.

The deed had been done. After a while, Harvey and I couldn't keep our hands off one another, but to be fair, we did try to stop many times because we felt bad about what we were doing. You made it so easy to continue because you wouldn't stop cheating on me. About six months after Harvey and I started having an affair, I found out that I was five months pregnant. I knew the baby was Harvey's baby because you'd spent so much of your time and energy cheating on me that in the span of time Harvey and I were having sex, you hadn't touched me... not even once. You were so busy with Carla, and of course, Robyn, that you didn't have any energy left for me. Once I found out that I was pregnant, I seduced you so I could pin the baby on you, since Harvey was adamant about me not having an abortion. When I told you that I was two months pregnant, I was really five months pregnant. When Robyn died, I was nine months pregnant, and even though her death was a tragedy, she gave me the perfect gift: an opportunity to have my son without your knowledge. My sister, Ravyn, and I had just reconciled because of Robyn's death. She was the one who came up with the plan. I would go to Mexico to visit her and help get Robyn's affairs in order. I simply told you I was going to Mexico to spend a few weeks with my other sister and you didn't ask any questions. You were so excited about the idea of shacking up with Carla that you actually bought my ticket, packed my bags and gave me more than enough money for my trip. You didn't ask me what my sister's name was, and when I came back, you didn't ask to see one picture from my trip. As a matter of fact, when I called you and told you that I had a miscarriage, you didn't do like most husbands would have done: You didn't take off work and fly to Mexico to be at your wife's side. You were so caught up in the idea of being with Carla that another baby with me meant more child support to pay if you left. I knew that telling you our son had died was the best gift I could have ever given you. You didn't ask to see a copy of your own son's death certificate and you didn't ask where he was buried. You just didn't care! You made lying to you easy. I brought Henry back into the country and Harvey met me at my mother's house to collect him. I told you that I'd had a miscarriage because you didn't want the child anyway. Of course, Harvey wanted to be sure that Henry was his child and not yours, so he had a D.N.A. test done on him. The results confirmed what we already knew. The likelihood that Henry was Harvey's son was 99.9 percent. Harvey took his son in and we agreed to never tell you about our affair or our son. You should see him. He looks just like him. Harvey stayed close to you for the remainder of our marriage because he wanted me to leave you and marry him, but I refused. He told me every little dirty secret you had, and even though he was a decent man, I knew that marrying him would be no better than being married to you. You and I both know that Harvey had a reputation and I was sure to tell him everything you said about him. That's why Harvey stopped speaking to you once I divorced you. He stayed close to you because he wanted Henry to know his brothers, Melvin and Damien. But when you got Carla pregnant, Harvey gave me some of the best advice he could've ever given me.

He said that to protect our secret, I needed to get you to sign over your rights to our sons; that way, when the children started getting to know one another, you wouldn't have access to them to find out about Henry. The choice was... let you be a not-so-present force in the children's lives or remove you and let them have a relationship with their brother. The choice was easy. You wouldn't be a great role model to them, plus, it was common sense that you'd only come around when you wanted to use your children to get to me. After all, you didn't have anything to do with Jessica or Jeff Jr. once you walked out of Brianna's life. You didn't even want to give Brianna any child support for those kids because you were a self-centered and self-absorbed individual and I wasn't about to let you take me and my kids through what you took

Brianna and her kids through. So, yes... I betrayed you more than once. I was to you what you were to me, only worse. And guess what? That's only half the story. Trust me, you couldn't handle the rest of it. If you don't want to end up on a milk carton, I suggest that you leave me and my kids alone. Walk away, Jeff, and don't look back because the day I see my son crying over you again is the day your family reports you missing."

With that, Naomi walked away from her surprised and tearful ex-husband. Jeff watched as Naomi got into her car. As she was lowering her body into the car, she gave Jeff the most evil glare he'd ever seen. It was at that moment that Jeff realized that demons were real. He didn't know if he was dreaming or not, but what he did know was he needed to change his life and fast. Naomi was so cold that she stood still for five minutes and detailed how she betrayed him, and not one time had she blinked or taken her eyes off Jeff. She was the very definition of evil and Jeff could feel a tugging on his broken soul. On one hand, he wanted to go after the wretched Naomi and destroy her, but on the other hand, he knew that he needed to stay far away from Naomi and any child that was born to her.

Jeff went back inside the gym to collect his things. His mind was racing and his heart felt like it was about to beat its way through his chest. He was hurt. He was experiencing more pain than he'd ever experienced. He'd been hurt before, but not like this. He'd been angry before, but not like this. He didn't focus on the concerned guys who asked him if he was okay. He walked right past them, gathered his things and walked out of the gym stunned. As he entered his vehicle, Jeff realized that for the first time in his life, his face was covered with tears. He couldn't stop crying. How could a human being be so evil? Jeff pulled out of the parking lot and onto the highway, but his mind was distracted by the revelation Naomi had just given him. The sound of someone holding their car's horn snapped Jeff back to reality. He was driving in two lanes at once. He snatched the wheel so hard that he hit the gravel and almost lost control of his car. He was able to regain control and he steered his vehicle back onto the road. Confused and scared, he headed back to his hotel room.

## Chapter 5

# The Wake Up Call

It was late, but Jeff found himself unable to sleep because he kept thinking of the confrontation he had with his son and Naomi earlier. His life was a mess. He'd hurt people and he'd been hurt by people. More than anything, he'd hurt his children and it wasn't until Melvin confronted him that he realized the extent of pain he'd caused his offspring.

Jeff finally began to doze off to sleep around three o'clock that morning and that's when he found himself in the middle of one of the worst nightmares he'd ever had. In the dream, Jeff was in a room with about eight or nine beautiful women. Every woman was wearing a two piece bathing suit. In the dream, Jeff was excitedly trying to unbutton his pants as he watched each woman pull on the strings of their bikini tops. Jeff's enthusiasm was cut short when, instead of removing their bikini tops, each woman had removed her skin, revealing a hideous, demon-like creature. Jeff tried to run, but there were three doors in front of him. He didn't know which door was the right one, so he chose the middle door. When he opened it, a very alive Robyn stepped through it and started trying to seduce him, but he was afraid of her. "You're dead," he screamed as Robyn began to pull on the strings to her bikini top. Jeff turned to the first door and opened it, but instead of a woman coming through that door, he saw a room with a casket in it. In the room, there were many people oblivious to his presence. Jeff's son, Melvin, walked up to the casket and opened it, and to Jeff's horror, he saw what appeared to be his lifeless body in the casket.

Horrified, Jeff ran to the third door, and this time, he saw clouds and he heard what sounded like angels singing. There was a calming peace coming from that door, so Jeff ran through it. It was then that he suddenly woke up. Sitting up in his bed, Jeff realized that he was covered in sweat and his heart was racing. He looked over at the clock, but it was obvious that the power had gone off and come back on while he was sleeping. Nevertheless, it was still dark outside, so Jeff decided to lie back down. Looking over at the nightstand, Jeff saw the empty beer bottle that he'd left there the night before. Jeff wasn't an alcoholic, but he did enjoy an occasional drink. He stretched his hand towards the bottle and knocked it off the nightstand. "I'm done drinking," he said as he lay back down. It wasn't long before Jeff drifted back off to sleep and found himself having another nightmare.

In this dream, Jeff could hear the prayers of a woman. Her voice was familiar, but it was obvious that her heart was broken. Jeff found himself in a big, empty room, but the sounds of prayer were coming from the other side of the wall he was closest to. There were no doors in the room; there was only one window that led into the other room. Jeff peered in through the window and saw a woman kneeling next to her bed. She was crying and praying for God to change her husband. Jeff's heart went out to the distressed soul, but he could not see her face. He wanted to go and comfort the woman, so he climbed through the window and made his way towards her. "Ma'am, are you okay?" he asked, but the woman obviously couldn't hear or see him. He walked to the other side of the bed so he could face the woman, but when he turned to look at her, his heart broke.  He suddenly realized he was in the bedroom he'd once shared with his first wife, Brianna, and the prayers were coming from Brianna herself.

There was a large television a few feet away from Brianna, and on the screen played the life of a younger Jeff.  Brianna would stop praying for a few seconds and watch Jeff as he went from one woman to the other, and then, she'd cry out in prayer again.  "Please stop him from cheating on me, Lord.  I'll do anything.  I love him.  Please don't let me lose my marriage!  Don't let me lose my marriage, God!  Please!  I will do anything!  I love my husband!  Please don't let me lose him!"  Brianna's voice grew louder and louder as her inner pain made its way out of her mouth.  Jeff's heart broke as he watched the wife of his youth plead with God to save her marriage.  Suddenly, Brianna picked up the remote control and changed the channel.  On the next channel, the word "Judgment" flashed across the screen as if it were the title of a horror movie. A few seconds later, the sound of traffic could be heard and the television screen flashed to a busy street in Los Angeles. It was the street where Jeff's first job was located. A pair of beautiful, long legs walked by and began to head towards Jeff's job. The woman was wearing red heels and a short black skirt. As she got closer to the door of the pizza shop where Jeff was working, it was obvious who she was. It was Naomi. Jeff watched the screen as a beautiful and seductive Naomi made her way into the shop. At that moment, he heard Brianna giggling as she placed the remote on her bed. Jeff looked at his ex-wife and saw that she was no longer crying over him. Instead, she let out a sigh of relief and uttered, "Amen" before turning off the television. Suddenly, Jeff was awakened from his sleep by the piercing sound of the hotel's alarm clock.

When he'd woken up a few hours earlier in
the middle of the night, the display on the
clock had been flashing, indicating that the
power had likely gone out and come back on.
Now, somehow, the correct time was
showing on the clock's display and the
display was not flashing. Jeff also noticed
that the beer bottle he knocked over the
night before was sitting on the nightstand in
the same spot it was in when he knocked it
over. It was then that Jeff realized he hadn't
truly woken up, but instead, he'd likely
dreamed that he'd woken up, and then, he'd
drifted into another nightmare. Scared, Jeff
looked over at the time. It was ten o'clock on
a Sunday morning and he was determined to
go to somebody's church. He didn't care
where he went. He knew that he needed God
and he needed Him fast. He'd witnessed
some scary stuff over the last few days and
Jeff knew that it would only get worse if he
didn't seek help. He called his golfing buddy,

Frankie, and canceled his golf plans so he could go to church.

Jeff didn't know what church to go to, so he planned to stop at the first one he saw. He prayed as he drove around the city looking for a church to visit. "Lord, I know I haven't talked to you in a long time. I know that I've done some really messed up things and I'm asking you for your forgiveness. I want to turn my life around, but I don't know where to start. I'm only in town for a few days, but I need to visit a church where your Spirit is. Please lead me to the church you want me to go to. Amen."

A few minutes later, Jeff came across a huge, dome-like church named Empowerment Kingdom Messianic Ministries. He'd heard about it a few years back after the church's pastor had passed away and there was a lot of speculation as to who would be his

successor. Jeff pulled into the parking lot of
the church where he was guided to an
available parking space by some of the
church's parking lot attendants. He was
thirty minutes late for service, but he didn't
care. He needed the Word of God and he
needed prayer, and at that moment, that's all
that mattered to him. With his head low, Jeff
walked into the church, where he was led to
the second level since the first level was full.

Pastor Elijah Simpson preached a powerful
sermon that sounded as if it had been custom
written for Jeff. He spoke on the power of
prayer and the effects that prayer and
fasting have against the kingdom of
darkness. He talked about demons, warfare
and deliverance. Jeff was by no means
ignorant of the Bible, after all, his
grandfather had been a pastor and Jeff was
raised by his grandparents.

As the service neared closing, Jeff had already made his mind up. He knew that he couldn't join the church because he lived in Arizona, but he was definitely going to rededicate his life to the Lord and ask for prayer. When the pastor gave the altar call, he was one of the first people to stand. One of the ushers signaled to Jeff to follow him and he led him down to the altar.

The line at the altar wrapped around the first floor. It was so long that Jeff wondered if the pastor would have enough time to truly pray for him. When he noticed that the pastor was prophesying and praying for some of the people in the line, he thought to himself that there was no way the pastor would get to him, or if he did, he'd be too tired or too empty to truly pray for him. Because of this, Jeff began to look behind himself to see if he could get out of the line. The line was long and there was no way that Jeff could slip by unnoticed, but he was willing to take his chances. He reasoned within his heart that he could probably find a small church where he'd get the personalized attention he believed he needed. Just when he was about to get out of line, the pastor said something that stopped him in his tracks. "Wait. There's somebody in this line who is ready to walk out. Don't get out of this line. You're not here by accident. I may not know your struggle, but God does and He's not too busy for you. Stay where you are and be patient with God." Chills ran down through Jeff's body as he received that message. He turned back around and stood still, patiently awaiting his turn to be prayed for. Wearing a black leather jacket, a black muscle top and blue jeans made Jeff somewhat uncomfortable. He noticed that the majority of the congregation wore semi-formal attire, and some of the younger guys wore polo style shirts, khaki pants and dress shoes.

Nevertheless, regardless of how he was dressed, Jeff knew that he needed to see the pastor.

Thirty minutes later, he found himself standing in front of the pastor. With the pastor, stood seven men who gathered around everyone he prayed for. They caught anyone who fell out after they were prayed for. Alongside the pastor were three women: his mother, his wife and his wife's armor bearer. At first, Jeff didn't pay attention to them. He focused on the pastor as he began to pray for him. "You were the one who was ready to get out of line. Am I right?" asked Pastor Elijah. Jeff nodded his head in affirmation. He wouldn't lift his head because of the hurt and shame he felt. He felt as if the pastor could see through the windows of his soul and peer directly into his life. The pastor began to prophesy to Jeff, telling him that he'd spent his entire life searching for a love that he didn't understand, and in his quest to find it, he'd hurt many people and he'd been hurt by many people. "God has forgiven you," said Pastor Elijah. "Now, you've got to forgive yourself." Jeff slowly began to lift his head, revealing his tear-stained cheeks. "There have been eight demons tormenting you, but today, that ends," said the pastor. "God said He's going to use you, but you've got to surrender your life to Him once and for all." Applause erupted in the crowded auditorium as Jeff began to lift his hands and lower his body to his knees. Jeff rededicated his life to the Lord, and when the pastor began to pray for him, he collapsed onto the floor, releasing the tormenting spirits that had been ruling his life.

Twenty minutes later, he regained consciousness, only to find that most of the congregation had retired to their seats. A few people still lie on the floor and the people were praising God, speaking in tongues and dancing around the church. There was a peace there... a peace that Jeff had never experienced before. As he tried to lift his weary body from the floor, three men came and assisted him. "Take a seat over here," said one of the men. "After service, you'll just follow us to the back for more prayer and encouragement." Jeff nodded his head in affirmation and made his way to the seat.

## Chapter 6

# The Prodigal Son

Service continued for another twenty minutes before the pastor asked everyone to stand to their feet for the final prayer. The pastor grabbed his wife's hands and just when they were about to lower their heads, Jeff recognized the first lady. It was Brianna, his ex wife! Jeff was shocked, but at the same time, he was relieved because she looked happy... very happy. She'd aged a little, but she'd grown even more beautiful with age. Everyone in the church had bowed their heads, but Jeff was looking around to see if his daughter, Jessica, or his son, Jeff Jr., were in the church. Once he realized that the pastor had started the prayer, he lowered his head, but his mind kept racing. What if Brianna and Pastor Elijah thought he'd purposely come into the church to start some type of dissension? Did the good pastor know who he was before he prayed for him? Had Brianna noticed him? Were his children in the church and had they seen or recognized him? Just when his thoughts were getting the best of him, he heard the pastor say, "Amen", and then, the congregation followed his lead and said, "Amen."

"Follow me," the usher said while gently placing his hand on Jeff's shoulder. Before Jeff could respond, the usher began to lead him towards an already formed line of people who were heading to the back for more prayer. Jeff wasn't sure if he wanted to follow the man, but he did and he found himself in a medium-sized room, seated in a folding chair alongside about forty other people. The people were being called out of the room one-by-one, and of course, the married were being led out together into separate prayer rooms where the prayer team ministered and prayed for them. Jeff contemplated getting up and leaving because he felt uncomfortable. He didn't want Brianna to think he was stalking her and he didn't want her husband to think that he'd come to his church to start a fight. To make matters worse, the ushers intentionally skipped over Jeff, making him the last person to be called.

"Mr. Spencer? Will you please follow me?" The voice was firm, but calming. Jeff rose to his feet and followed the somewhat stout man into another room. When Jeff entered the meeting room, he immediately locked eyes with Brianna. He hesitated at the door and considered leaving, but Brianna's warm smile relaxed him a little.

"Please, take a seat," said Pastor Elijah. "It's

nice to finally meet you, Jeff."

Jeff felt ashamed. "I'm sorry," he said. "I didn't know that..."

"No apologies needed," responded the good pastor. "God sent you here. My apologies. I asked them to let us see everyone else first because I knew our meeting would probably be long... or short; that's entirely up to you. I didn't want you to feel rushed out, but if it makes you feel better, I was adamant that they not let you leave." With that, Pastor Elijah smiled and extended his hand towards the chair next to Jeff.

After hearing Pastor Elijah's words, Jeff felt comfortable enough to sit down.

"Honestly, I'm not sure if I feel comfortable enough sharing my problems with you, but I do believe the Lord led me here. First off, pastor, with your permission, I would love to address Brianna here."

"No problem, man... Go ahead."

"Brianna. I've made a mess of my life. I made a lot of mistakes in my life and one of the biggest regrets I have is how I treated you and my children. I was a lousy husband, father and just a lousy person all around, and for that, I offer you my sincerest apologies."

Brianna's warm smile hadn't changed. "It's okay," she said. "I've forgiven you a long time ago and I know that you were just in a dark place, but I always knew that God would call you out of that darkness and use you someday. I just want you to know that I have forgiven you and I always made sure to uplift you to the kids, so they don't hold any anger towards you either. With that, I know that you're not here for a family reunion, so I'll just leave you two and we'll talk before you leave... if you want to. No rush."

Jeff was amazed at Brianna's love and

humility. She had always been a beautiful and loving spirit, but when he was in his darkest hour, he couldn't see that. "Thank you. Yes, we'll chat before I leave." Brianna left the room so the men could talk.

"This is awkward," said Jeff as he dropped his head.

"It's okay. Listen. I've been married before as well. I have a beautiful sixteen year old daughter with my ex-wife. My ex, Brenda, has remarried and all of us have a really good relationship because of our daughter. I'm not here to judge you, brother."

"Yeah, that kinda caught me off guard. I came here because I've been experiencing some weird stuff these last few days. I definitely wasn't expecting this."

"What happened?"

"Well, as you probably already know...

some years ago, I divorced Brianna and married a woman I'd been seeing. Well, that woman's name was Naomi, and for a long time, I thought she was a fairly decent woman. I'd seen a few red flags here and there, but I chalked it up to her being a woman... you know."

*Pastor Elijah laughed.* "Trust me. I do understand."

"Anyhow, I was the same man with Naomi that I'd been with Brianna... probably worse. I did what I knew how to do. I cheated. Naomi had a friend named Carla and I cheated with Carla. Naomi found out and left. So, here's where things got weird. I went to Naomi's mother's house some years back trying to... you know... fix things. Some dude came out of nowhere and slugged me. I didn't know who he was or why he'd punched me, but a bunch of guys came and grabbed him before I could get off the ground.  A few minutes later, Naomi came out the house and told me that the guy, who's name is Duke, by the way, was the husband of her dead sister, Robyn.  She said that I was responsible for her sister's death.  That's when she started showing me a bunch of photos of a woman I'd met probably about a year or two prior to that incident.  I didn't know the woman was Naomi's sister.  I didn't know Naomi had a sister named Robyn.  Anyhow, I learned that Robyn had died in a car accident trying to get away from her husband after he'd caught her coming out of a hotel with me.  I messed up real bad.  Naomi asked me for a divorce and I couldn't argue with her, because again, I'd messed up real bad.  She manipulated me into signing over my paternal rights. I was making close to six figures back then and my money was the most

important thing to me at that time. I
know it was foolish, but I was a young
cat back then. I went ahead and married
Carla because she was pregnant and I
didn't want to pay child support. I'm
just being honest here; after all, we are
in the house of the Lord. So, anyway, a
year later, Carla and I separated and
that's when I decided to look up my ex,
Naomi. I found her on Facebook and it
turned out that she'd married her dead
sister's husband, Duke."

"What?"

"Yep. True story. So, I was angry. I felt
betrayed. I was looking at all the photos
she'd posted up of this man raising my
sons and I got angry. I wrote her a
message on Facebook and she
manipulated me yet again. Naomi
always knew how to silence me. It's
funny. I spent years married to that
woman, thinking I was good at

manipulating her, but that wasn't the case. I was dealing with a woman who was a master manipulator. Compared to her, I was just a rookie. Anyhow, I didn't pursue the matter because I was freshly separated from Carla and I'd just lost my job. I didn't have the energy or the resources to go after Naomi. Now, let's fast forward. I just arrived in town a few days ago from Arizona... that's where I live now. I decided to go to a new gym up on Rozelle Avenue and that's where I ran into my son, Melvin. Imagine my surprise when I saw my own son after all these years. Just as I was approaching him, I heard Naomi's voice. I turned around and when she saw me, she looked like she'd seen a ghost. My son, Melvin, wants nothing to do with me and when Naomi saw how angry Melvin had gotten, she came to me and started telling me all kinds of secrets... stuff I wouldn't have dreamed of in my darkest hour. She told me that the baby I thought she'd miscarried was alive, and get this... he is the son of my ex best-friend! I mean, this man was my mentor... a man I trusted with my life. It turned out that Naomi went to Mexico to have the baby, and then, she told me she'd had a miscarriage. I believed her. I didn't think she'd have any reason to lie about that because it was clear that she wasn't pregnant anymore. I was so caught up in myself and what I wanted at that time that I didn't think to ask questions. Well, as it turns out... that baby is alive. She brought it... I mean him... back to the United States and gave him to my best friend to raise. This guy called me and told me that some woman he'd had a one night stand with had given birth to a son and was about to give him up for adoption. He said that he went to the hospital, had a blood test done and the boy was his, so he took custody of him. He didn't tell me that he'd had a baby by my wife. This man sat in my house, ate at my table, played with my children, and as it turns out, slept with my wife. Back to the story though. When Naomi was going off on me, I saw something dark in her. The way she looked at me... it was like I was looking straight at the devil, himself. Anyhow, to sum it all up, she pretty much threatened my life. She stood right there, looked me in my eyes and threatened my life. The way she looked at me sent chills down my spine. When she walked off, I couldn't take my eyes off her. I didn't realize I was crying. Look at me... I'm crying now, just talking about it. She turned around and gave me the coldest look I'd ever seen and I know I saw the devil. I didn't believe in

demons until I saw the devil in her. I
went home that night, had a beer and
went to sleep. That's when I had one of
the scariest nightmares ever, and the
second nightmare I had was about
Brianna. I hope this doesn't make you
uncomfortable."

"No. Of course not. Go ahead."

"I dreamed that I walked into our old
bedroom and I could see and hear
Brianna, but she couldn't see or hear me.
She was crying and praying. It broke my
heart. She was praying for God to save
our marriage. She kept stopping to
watch television..."

"Television?"

"Yep, but she wasn't watching a movie.
She was watching me go out in the
streets and mess around with a bunch of
women. She kept pausing the movie of
my life to pray some more. Then, she
changed the channel and I saw the word,

"Judgment" flash on the screen. That's when I saw Naomi walking towards my old job. I used to work at a pizza shop and I met Naomi when I was working at that place. What's amazing is that she was wearing the same thing she'd worn the day I met her, and get this... I didn't remember what she'd worn until I saw it in the dream! So, now, I'm freaking out and I know this demon stuff is real. I gotta give my life back to God. I just have to."

Pastor Elijah sat up straightway in his seat. "Wow. Yeah. Whew. That is quite the story. I've been pastoring for about ten years now and I thought I'd heard it all, but I was wrong. No offense, brother, but that's a doozy. Let me get this straight because I'm at a loss for words. So, your ex wife, Naomi was pregnant... right? She went to Mexico and came

back with a flat stomach and no baby?
She told you that she'd had a
miscarriage, but the baby was actually
alive."

"Henry."

"Okay, so Henry was the baby's name?"

"Yeah."

"So, Naomi went off to another country
to give birth to your best friend's baby."

"My best friend and mentor..."

"Okay. Wow. So, she had the baby but
told you that she'd miscarried him...
right? In truth, she'd given the baby to
your best friend... and mentor, and this
guy continued to call you, pretending
that one of his old flings had pretty much
just dropped a baby in his lap. Did I get
that right?"

"Pretty much."

"Yeah, man. You were married to a she-
devil. That wasn't a woman; that was a
devil. Like I said, I've been pastoring for

a little over ten years now and I've never heard anything like that and I've heard everything. Well, brother; first off, let me tell you to stop beating yourself up. We all have a past. Some of us have decent past; some of us have bad pasts, and some of us have pasts that nobody can seem to forget. Let me tell you... For me, I haven't always been a pastor. There was a time when I wasn't right and my folks were in church. I was in the church, married to my first wife and expecting my first child and I thought I was being robbed of everything life had to offer. I was living a cozy life trying to make my parents proud and I got tired of being safe. I got tired of being the church boy, so I went out there and cheated on my wife with just about any and every woman who looked halfway decent. I was gambling, experimenting with drugs, going in and out of jail... I was wild. Anyhow, Brenda, my first wife, was losing her mind trying to find some kind of way to get me to settle down. She told my parents every time I messed up. She went to the church board on me. She even told a few of my co-workers what I had been doing. I lost my job behind that woman. I was angry with her. I was so angry with her that I began to hate her. That's when I got real nasty. I started bringing women in our house and sleeping with them in our bed when she was at work. I didn't care who saw me bringing those women into my house either. When I look back now, I realize that I was really trying to send a message to my parents, the church, my wife... to anybody who would hear. I wanted them all to know that I was going to be my own man, make my own mistakes and live my own life. A few years into our marriage and Brenda had

had enough. She knew I wasn't going to let her leave easily, so she called a woman I had been messing with... a woman everybody called Apple. Apple was one of those women who would mess with married men, and then, reach out to their wives and tell them every gruesome detail of the affair. What I didn't know was that Brenda had forged a friendship with Apple, and even though the two women didn't like each other, they had a common enemy: me. Apple was mad at me for ending our affair and Brenda was mad at me for having an affair. Anyhow, Apple knew that I wasn't serious about leaving her alone, so she called me one Saturday morning and asked me if I'd ride to Vegas with her. She said that she'd already booked a room at a fancy hotel and everything was paid for. She said some things to me to motivate me, and of course, I won't mention them, but anyway, I told Brenda that I was about to head out of town to help an old friend move to Los Angeles. I should have known that something was wrong because she agreed too easily. She didn't ask any questions. She didn't fight with me at all. She just asked me what time I thought I'd be in the following day, and I think I told her around three or four. It wasn't until I got halfway to Las Vegas that I began to get suspicious. There was something different about Apple. She wasn't angry with me and she wasn't talking too much along the way. I thought about the two of them pairing up, but I brushed it off because Brenda was one of those good girls. She couldn't hurt a fly. We got to Vegas and Apple treated me to the time of my life. Everything seemed to be going perfectly, but I got worried because Brenda wasn't picking up the house phone when I called and that wasn't like her. Well, needless to say, I didn't enjoy my trip too much because something just felt off. I insisted on driving back to California because I wanted to get on I-15 and punch the gas. When I got home, my worst fears were confirmed. Brenda had packed up and left. She took everything with her except my clothes. Wait... she did take some of the clothes she'd bought for me. I started suspecting that Apple was involved when she kept calling me and asking where I was. Apple didn't normally do that. Well, anyway... I got confirmation when I finally spoke to Brenda. She'd moved back to Alabama and she told me that if I came after her or Eliyah, our daughter, she was going to have a few billboards made of the pictures Apple had sent her. She told me where Apple and I had stayed. She told me what I wore, how many times we had sex and she told me about some of the conversations Apple and I had. She said she was going to post those billboards in front of my parents' church. You see, even though Apple and Brenda were different, they knew how to put their differences behind them to get what they wanted. Apple wanted me, but Brenda didn't want me anymore, so they worked together to get what they wanted. In the end, I wanted Brenda back, but she wouldn't have me, and Apple wanted me back, but I wouldn't have anything to do with her. Brenda and I divorced, and at first, she didn't want me anywhere near Eliyah. But after my parents spoke with us, she agreed to giving me supervised visitations until I proved myself to be mature enough to have weekend visitations. My parents told me in no uncertain terms that if I didn't straighten up and fly right, they were going to pay to help Brenda get one of the best attorneys in the country. They said they would help her get full custody of Eliyah and they'd testify against me that I was not fit to have unsupervised visits with Eliyah. I was livid. After all, everybody knew my parents. My dad was well-known and everybody loved my mother. My dad was friends with just about every judge in Los Angeles! I couldn't expect a fair case. I agreed to their terms and I started growing up when I realized that I wasn't going to be able to see some of the most important events of my daughter's life... all because of my immaturity. I say that to encourage you, my brother. Every last one of us has a past. I'm not proud of my past, but I can honestly say that the path I took was necessary because it woke me up. If I hadn't gone through everything I've gone through, I wouldn't have ever taken God, life, marriage or fatherhood seriously. You probably had to deal with Naomi because of the level of deception you were walking in. You needed a big devil to help you realize that there is an even bigger God. It got your attention, didn't it? You're sitting here right now because the devil you once served took off its mask and showed you its face. That's why I tell parents to this day to stop trying to force their children to go down the paths they've planned for them to go on and just let God order their steps. I tell you that when God orders your steps, He will allow you to follow the enemy down some dark paths because He understands that it's your lack of knowledge and those hidden desires that led you to that mindset in the first place. He'll let you follow the wrong people and do the wrong things because He knows you're searching for something... something you're not going to find on the path you're on. He'll let you meet up with folks more wicked than yourself because when you're walking in darkness, you don't understand the light, so whenever someone who's saved, sanctified and filled with the Holy Spirit tries to minister to you, you'll stiffen your neck at them. But when the darkness starts to consume you and the evil you love starts to show you how much it hates you, you will find yourself running for your life while in the darkness. I don't mean to preach to you, but I have to tell you that when you're in the darkness and God suddenly turns the lights on to let you see what you've been following, it is then and only then that you'll come to understand that demons are real. When you know that demons are real, you'll know that God is real. Some folks are led to the light by the light, while others are chased into the light by the evils that reside in the darkness. But I'll tell you this... the ones who are playing in the darkness when the lights suddenly come on often turn out to be some of the most God-fearing and faithful servants to ever pick up a microphone. They can testify of the evils in this world because they've not only seen the light, but they've personally witnessed what's hidden in the darkness."

The conversation between Pastor Elijah and Jeff went on for another fifteen minutes, before the door opened and Brianna interrupted. "Remember, we have a lunch date with the Bowmans in thirty minutes," she said, pointing at the watch on her arm. Jeff rose to his feet.

"Well, I need to be getting back to my hotel room.  It was more than a pleasure and I want to say to you from one father to another, thank you for being there for my children when I wasn't man enough to do it myself, and thank you for encouraging me on today.  I truly appreciate you, brother.  Please keep me in prayer.  I'm going to need a lot of it."

"No problem.  And I'll let you tell Brianna what we talked about.  I really look forward to getting to know you and we will definitely be praying for you.  I know that all will work out for your good."

As the guys exited the room, they saw Brianna standing outside the door talking with Mrs. Peterson, the head deacon's wife.  "Excuse us," said Brianna to Mrs. Peterson.  "I'll talk with you later."  She turned to face Jeff who she could tell had lived a really rough life.  His pores had gotten bigger and

his once smooth skin looked somewhat
rough. Far from the ruggedly handsome man
he once was, Jeff had managed to maintain
his muscular physique. He was still
somewhat handsome, in Brianna's opinion,
but life hadn't dealt him the best hand.

"So, what were you two talking about?"
Brianna asked jokingly.

"I'll let you two talk," said Pastor Elijah
as he attempted to walk away.

"No, I want you right here," said Jeff.
"You're the husband, so the two of you
are one. I respect what you've done over
the years and I don't ever want to cut
you out of the picture when I've been out
of it intentionally myself."

Pastor Elijah turned around and nodded his
head. Jeff looked at Brianna again.

"Brianna, I want to apologize again for
the man I've been over the years. We've
gotten past the husband part. I see that
God let a man find you who was more

worthy of your heart, but I want to especially apologize for the father I've been... or haven't been. I guess I've just been walking around sleeping all these years and I can't promise to be the best father, but what I can say is if you'll let me, I'd like to try to be a decent father."

"Of course, Jeff. I could never cut you out of your children's lives. Regardless of our past, they love you. I have never spoken a bad word about you to them because they are a part of you, so telling them that you are bad would have been the same as telling them that they were partly bad or predisposed to do the wrong thing. I knew you'd reach out to them one day and I'm just happy to see you making a turn for the better, not just for the kids, but for you."

"Thanks. I was talking with Mr. Simpson here..."

"Call me Elijah."

"Okay, I was talking with Elijah and I want to share with you what I said to him. I don't want the kids to see me like this. I have a long ways to go and I want to make sure that I won't come into their lives and hurt them again. I don't know if it'll take me a few weeks, a few months or a few years to get myself together, but what I do know is I want a relationship with them. Please keep praying for me and be patient with me as I find myself a church home in Arizona and I try to navigate through the mess I've made with my life. Mr. Simpson... I mean Elijah has given me a list of churches to check out and I'm going to be praying and seeing where God leads me."

"I understand and I respect you for that. We'll definitely be praying for you on this end. Did Elijah give you our number?"

"Yes, I have it. I'll definitely be in touch."

*"If the righteous is repaid on earth, how much more the wicked and the sinner!"*
(Proverbs 11:31/ ESV)

## Chapter 7

# A Father's Love

Over the next few months, Jeff kept in touch with Elijah and Brianna. Their budding friendship was valuable to Jeff. Additionally, Jeff began attending one of the churches Elijah recommended. He continued to grow in the Lord, and even though he was a babe in Christ, Jeff began to hunger for God all the more. Four months after Jeff rededicated his life to the Lord, he felt he was ready to see his children with Brianna. He'd made up his mind that he was going all the way with God and he told himself that regardless of the obstacles he would face in his life, he was not going to turn back to the life God had called him out of. During their conversations, Brianna had told Jeff that Jeff Jr. was in his first year of medical school and Jessica was in a personal storm of her own.

It was the dead of winter, and Christmas was quickly approaching. After speaking with Elijah and Jessica, Jeff made up his mind to spend the Christmas holidays in Los Angeles so he could reunite with his children. Jeff was excited about seeing the children that he hadn't seen in almost two decades. He worried about how they would receive him and he worried that Elijah would feel threatened by his relationship with them. After all, Elijah had pretty much been the only father they knew, and Jeff understood that. He respected Elijah and didn't want to make him feel uncomfortable with his sudden presence in their lives, but Elijah was far from threatened. He was happy that Jeff was in the children's lives because he selflessly loved Jeff's children as if they were his own. He wanted them to be happy and he wanted them to know that their happiness meant far more to him than his own pride.

Christmas Eve finally arrived and Jeff was nervously pacing back and forth in his hotel suite. He'd arrived in Los Angeles the previous day and he was more than anxious to get the first meeting over with. He was excited about seeing his children, and he was nervous about the surprise Elijah and Brianna said they had for him. He hadn't bought them a Christmas present because he didn't know what to give the couple who he believed had everything, so he opted to give them a five hundred dollar gift card instead. Elijah had arranged to pick Jeff up at his room around six o'clock that evening so they could surprise the children at supper. When Elijah arrived to pick Jeff up, he found him nervously pacing in front of the hotel. He parked his car and walked over to Jeff to offer him some encouraging words. He knew that he was afraid, not just of how his children would see him, but Jeff was afraid that he'd hurt or disappoint them again. After encouraging him in the Lord, Elijah led him back to his running car and the men headed to Elijah's house.

"What's my surprise?" asked Jeff inquisitively. Elijah giggled. "You'll see in a few minutes."

By the time the men arrived, Brianna had already set the table for dinner. Jessica and Jeff Jr. were seated at the table, anxiously waiting for Elijah to return with their surprise. The couple's other children (Ezra, Lily and Miles) were also seated. They'd all thought that Elijah was heading to the church to pick up whatever gifts he'd stashed for them there, but they were wrong. "Honey, I'm home!" Elijah said jokingly as he locked

the living room door behind him. Jeff
nervously followed Elijah through the living
room wondering if he was about to receive
the same reaction from Jeff Jr. as he'd
received from his son, Melvin. Jeff Jr. was the
first to see Jeff as he rounded the corner into
the dining room. Without hesitation, he
sprung from his seat and rushed towards his
father. "Is it really you, Dad? It's you; isn't
it?!" He picked Jeff up and spun around with
him in his arms, all the while, repeatedly
screaming, "It's really you!" Jeff Jr. was tall
like his dad and he was the spitting image of
his father. He cried all the more when Jeff
wrapped his arms around him and hugged
him tightly. "I'm so sorry, son," said Jeff. "I
will never walk out of your life again." The
moment was so captivating and warm that
Jeff almost forgot about Jessica, who was now
seated tearfully at the table, staring at her
father. Ezra, Lily and Miles looked at Jessica.
"He is your dad," said Lily. "Give him another

chance." As the eldest of Jeff's children, Jessica remembered a lot of things about her father that she didn't like. She'd missed him, but she struggled with whether she should trust him or shun him. Jeff opened his tearful eyes and lovingly looked at his beautiful daughter. She was definitely her mother's child. She looked a lot like Brianna had looked at her age. Jessica pushed her seat back and slowly lifted her body from the seat, and that's when Jeff saw his surprise. Jessica was pregnant... she was very, very pregnant. She slowly made her way towards her father. Everyone in the room worried that Jessica was going to strike him, so the room was very quiet. After all, Jessica was the one who'd struggled the most with forgiving her father, not just for abandoning them, but for how he'd treated Brianna. Suddenly, Jessica was standing in front of her father, and without warning, she wrapped her arms around him and began to weep. Jeff felt a flood of emotions overwhelming him all at once. He felt love and compassion for his daughter and he felt relieved that she was willing to receive him back into her life.

Dinner in the Simpson household that night was better than delightful. Everyone laughed at the jokes that Elijah and Jeff told. They seemed to be in sync with one another. It was as if they were old friends catching up. Junior excitedly told his dad about his life's journey and how he'd decided upon a career in medicine. Jeff looked in awe at his well-mannered, well-spoken son. It was then that Jeff realized why he couldn't have been in his children's lives. He would have introduced them to a world that would have swallowed them up whole. Junior didn't talk like the guys where Jeff had come from. He didn't speak slang, nor was he obsessed with women. He was focused on his goals and he'd made a timeline for his life... one that included getting married at the age of 30 and having his first child by the age of 32. He was a well-rounded boy and Jeff was proud to call him his son. Jessica, on the other hand, had dropped out of college temporarily. She was the eldest, but she'd gotten married the previous year, and while eating supper, she tearfully updated her father about her marriage. She was separated from her husband, because like her father, he wasn't a one-woman man.

"So, what do you want to do about your marriage?" asked Jeff. His eyes were piercing and Jessica could tell that her father didn't want her to continue her marriage to Rory. "I love him," explained Jessica. "I do want our marriage to work, but I don't want a cheating man. It's hard, you know... because on one hand, I keep holding out and hoping that he'll change, but on another hand, it's like... I know better. Rory is Rory and he thinks he's God's gift to women."

"What does Rory want?"

"He wants to reconcile. I moved out last week and he's been calling me everyday begging me to come home, but I'm pregnant. This baby is due any day now and I can't be under any stress. I've decided to go back and give him one more chance, but I know he's going to blow it. He's supposed to be coming by tonight to pick me up."

"What time is he coming?"

Brianna recognized the look in Jeff's eyes. She motioned for her daughter to look her way, but when she couldn't get Jessica's attention, Brianna spoke up. "Oh no," she said laughing. "You are not about to intimidate that boy." Elijah interrupted, "Leave him alone. That's what fathers do. We intimidate." After speaking those words, Elijah glanced over at his daughter, Lily. "We intimidate every boy who dares to look at our offspring." Ezra and Miles giggled as Lily rolled her eyes at her father.

Just as they were speaking, the door bell rang. "May I do the honor?" Jeff asked Elijah. "You may," responded Elijah as he bowed and laughingly pointed towards the door. Jessica looked at her giggling mother. "You better stop him," said Brianna. "He's gonna scare that boy off." Jessica didn't care. She was tired of Rory's adulterous ways and she wanted him to straighten up or leave.

Jeff answered the door. "Come in, Rory," he said. Brianna and Elijah explained to Rory that Jeff was Jessica's biological father, and already, Rory knew he hadn't made a good first impression with Jeff. Everyone was talking with Rory as he stood near the front door... everyone but Jeff. Jeff spent the entire time scowling at the uncomfortable Rory, and without warning, Jeff interrupted.

"Excuse us, y'all.  Rory and I are about to take a ride."

Rory was afraid.  He'd heard so many bad things about Jeff.  "We are?" he asked sheepishly.  Jeff grabbed his coat from behind the door.  "We'll be back," he said.  Brianna wanted to stop Rory from leaving with Jeff, but Elijah reassured her that he would be okay.  "It's a man thing," Elijah said.  "Only a man knows how to speak with a man and Jeff has been where Rory is.  He knows how to reach him.  Trust me."

Jeff was gone with Rory for more than an hour.  Brianna was worried, but Jessica remained unusually calm.  When the men returned, a noticeably frightened Rory came into the house and asked Jessica if he could speak with her outside.  Jeff stepped inside the home as Rory and Jessica headed out the door.

"What did you say to him?  I've never seem

him this scared!  What did you say to him?" laughed Elijah.

"I told him the truth," said Jeff.  "I might have said a few more things too, but I don't want to repeat them, given this is a Christian household."

"Well, hopefully, he listens to you because I've been trying to get that boy to see the light for a long time now."

"Oh, trust me... He's heard me loud and clear, but the effects of what I said may be short-term.  I hot-wired him with the fear of Jeff to hold him over until you can put the fear of God in him.  Oh, by the way, I got his mistress, Zayana's phone number, address, job location, job description, parents' names and confession of faith.  Trust me, he couldn't call her back if he wanted to."

After Jessica and Rory spoke outside for about thirty minutes, Jessica made her way back into the house to bid her parents farewell.  Before she could say a word, she stopped and wrapped her arms around her father.  "I've missed you so much," she said.  "Please don't leave me again."  Jeff was humbled.  He'd spent his entire life looking for a love that he already had.  "I won't," he said.  "I now know how to love someone more than I love myself."

Two weeks after they met, Jessica gave birth to a baby girl she named London.  Brianna called Jeff and kept him abreast of his daughter and granddaughter's conditions.  Once London was born, Brianna sent Jeff a text message with London's picture inserted.  It read, "Congratulations, old man.  You are now the proud grandfather of a seven pound, five ounce baby girl.  A few days later, Jeff traveled back to Los Angeles to meet his granddaughter for the first time.

*"Behold, I give unto you power to tread on serpents and scorpions, and over all the power of the enemy: and nothing shall by any means hurt you."*
(Luke 10:19/ KJV)

# Chapter 8

## When Weapons are Formed

It had been a year since Jeff reconciled with Jessica and Jeff Jr. and the news had traveled fast about his conversion to Christianity. Jeff was heavily involved with the church, going out into the streets with his church to share the gospel. The news of Jeff's sudden change made its way to Naomi by way of her son, Melvin. Melvin had been monitoring Jeff's social network profiles and he was bothered by his father's sudden claim to salvation. Even more bothersome to Melvin were the pictures of Jeff spending time with Jessica and Jeff Jr. Melvin didn't know Jessica or

Junior personally, and seeing how easily they'd forgiven their father was troubling him. After all, Melvin despised his father and didn't want him to have any good things in his life. He wanted Jeff to suffer and he wanted him to suffer miserably.

Damien, on the other hand, wanted a relationship with Jeff. Seeing that Jeff had reconciled with Jessica and Jeff Jr. gave him hope, but he didn't tell his mother or brother about his desires to reconcile with his father. He knew how much they despised him and he didn't want them to turn their anger to him, so he pretended to hate his father as well.

Melvin was determined to ruin his father's name, so he devised a plan to reach out to him and pretend to want a relationship with him. His plan was to earn his father's trust so that he could travel down to Arizona and stay with him for a few days. While there, he planned to plant drugs in Jeff's car. Melvin wanted to make sure that Jeff was charged with a felony, so he decided to plant a lot of drugs in his vehicle. He would then call the police and leave an anonymous tip about the location of the drugs. He knew that Jeff had an extensive criminal history if he was arrested, he'd lose everything he'd worked so hard for in the last year. Jeff was now working at a new sales and marketing company and was quickly climbing the ladder of success; Melvin was jealous. Jeff was now in a relationship with a woman he'd met at church by the name of Tahir and it was clear that their blossoming romance was serious because Jeff often uploaded pictures of Tahir to his Facebook page. He would always refer to her as his blessing. Melvin told his mother, Naomi, about his plan, and even though she didn't encourage him to follow through with it, she didn't try to stop him either.  Secretly, Naomi wanted Melvin's plan to work because of her growing hatred and envy of Jeff.  Naomi didn't want Jeff to be happy either.  She wanted Tahir to leave Jeff's life and she knew that Melvin's plans to ruin his father's name would likely run Tahir off.  After all, Naomi had been checking Tahir's Facebook profile as well and she'd noticed that every one of Tahir's posts were about God.

Melvin followed through with his plan and reached out to his father on Facebook.  "It's taken me a long time to forgive you for abandoning us, but you appear to be a better person now.  I would love to get to know you better and I hope that you're open to getting to know me as well."  Melvin's note was short and to the point and Jeff was happy to read it.  Even though he was excited about the idea of getting to know Melvin and Damien again, he felt somewhat uneasy.  Nevertheless, in the spirit of fatherhood, he decided to open his life to his sons with Naomi.

Over the next month, Jeff spoke with Melvin and Damien at least once a week. Each time he'd spoken with them, he felt uneasy... especially because neither of the boys mentioned their mother, nor did he ever hear her in the background. "I'd love to come down to Arizona for about a week to catch up with you," said Melvin to his father. Jeff agreed, but he couldn't shake that uneasy feeling he had about Melvin. When he spoke with Damien, he wasn't uneasy, but there was something about Melvin that made Jeff want to pull away from him. Jeff told his concerns to his pastor and he also told Elijah and Brianna about them. They all said they would pray for Jeff.

The weekend that Melvin was supposed to drive to Arizona finally arrived and Jeff was in the grocery store loading his cart with food.  It had been an hour since Melvin called to inform him that he was thirty minutes away from Jeff's house, so Jeff hurriedly rushed towards the registers to pay for his food.  Suddenly, his cellular phone started ringing.  It was Damien and he was frantic.

"Hey Damien.  Slow down.  Tell me what's going on again."

"We just got a call saying that Melvin's been in a car accident!

"Car accident?!  Where is he?  How's he doing?"

"We don't know!  We're on our way to the airport now, but the doctors say that he isn't looking good!"

"I'm on my way!" yelled Jeff as he abandoned his shopping cart and rushed out of the store's doors.

When Jeff arrived at the hospital, he learned

that Melvin had run a red light and was hit by an eighteen wheeler truck. The doctors said he needed an immediate blood transfusion and Jeff eagerly offered his blood to his son. The police officers were also at the hospital and they informed Jeff that they'd found a large amount of cocaine and heroin in Melvin's car.

It was the middle of the night when Naomi and Damien burst through the emergency room's doors. Immediately, Naomi spotted Jeff, who was seated on the floor in what appeared to be a trance. "Where's Melvin?!" she screamed at Jeff. "Where's my baby?!" Jeff couldn't answer her. "Are you Melvin Spencer's mother?" It was the doctor. Naomi turned around and looked into the doctor's eyes. Before she could answer him, she noticed that the doctor was removing his scrub cap. "No!" screamed Naomi. "Where's my baby? Where's my baby?!" The doctor dropped his head. "Are you Melvin Spencer's mother? I need an answer before I can answer you." Jeff lifted himself from the floor. "Yes, she's his mother," he said. That's when the doctor spoke the words that took the breath out of Naomi. "I'm sorry ma'am. Your son expired at 10:42 pm. He had severe..."

Before the doctor could finish speaking, Naomi fainted. Damien sat down on the floor and began to weep. Staring at Damien from across the room, Jeff knew he couldn't sit by and watch his son grieve. He walked over to Damien and began to hug him. "I'm sorry," he said. "I'm so, so sorry."

An hour later, Naomi woke up in a hospital bed. Confused, she wanted to know why she was in the hospital and she demanded to see Melvin. The nurse explained to Naomi that she'd fainted after hearing about her son's death. Naomi tried to lift her weary body from the bed. "Where is he?!" she said loudly. "Where is Melvin? I want to see him now!" Jeff and Damien stood outside the door of Naomi's room and listened as Naomi berated the nurses and demanded to see her now deceased son. A few minutes later, two doctors went into the room to help restrain and sedate Naomi.

"How long did you know?" Jeff asked Damien. "For about two weeks now," responded Damien. "I heard Melvin and my mom talking one night and Melvin was really angry with you. He said something about you playing daddy to Brianna's kids and he said something about destroying you. That's when I heard my mom saying that you deserved it. I wanted to tell you, but I couldn't." Jeff nodded his head and wrapped his arms around his grieving son. "It's okay. It's not your fault," responded Jeff.

Jeff's phone suddenly rang. It was Elijah. Damien excused himself, saying that he needed to go and check on his mother. "I'll be in the lobby," said Jeff to Damien. "I'll be back in a few."

"Hey, brother."

"How are you holding up?"

"I think I'm still in shock, man. And to make matters worse, Damien just told me that Melvin was coming to Arizona to plant drugs on me. He and his mother had planned to ruin my reputation. I wouldn't have believed it if the officer hadn't told me that he'd found a large amount of drugs in Melvin's car."

"Are you serious?!"

"Yes, indeed. I told you that woman has it out for me."

"Yeah, you need to stay away from her... far, far away. She won't stop until she's destroyed you."

"What's crazy is all this time, she had me thinking that Melvin was my son, when he wasn't. Can you imagine my pain when the doctor told me that I couldn't give blood to my own son because we didn't have the same blood type? I know I haven't been around in Melvin's life much, but I still loved him."

"Well, that explains the uneasiness you said you had when you spoke with him and that explains why he hated you so much. I mean look at how easily Damien has taken to you."

"I guess you're right, but it doesn't stop it from hurting. Now, I want to know who his real father was."

"Me too. Seriously, man... You need to write a book."

"Tell me about it. Now, she's in the room screaming that she wants to see the boy, but she's the one responsible for his death. I mean if she had acted like a mother and told him that his plan was not a good idea, he'd be alive right now."

"That's right. Well, you know that you are protected by God. God wasn't going to let that boy hurt you. I hate to say it, but that's probably why he ended up the way he did."

"I don't doubt it, man."

"What about the other kid? What's his name... Damien?"

"Yeah, his name is Damien. I know he's mine. I can feel it. He looks like me. We have a powerful father/ son connection."

"Okay. Just know that we're praying for you on this end."

"Thanks. I really appreciate it."

A week after Melvin's death, the family held his funeral. Naomi's bitterness towards Jeff had grown into full-blown hatred. She not only wanted to see Jeff dead, she wanted to see him suffer a slow and agonizing death.

She learned through the doctors that Jeff had tried to give blood to Melvin, but his blood type didn't match Melvin's blood type. The doctors explained to Naomi that Jeff was not Melvin's biological father, and she agreed. She knew who Melvin's father was and she was all-too-eager to reveal his identity during the reception after Melvin's funeral. In her pain, Naomi was still determined to destroy Jeff by any means necessary.

During the reception, a familiar, but older man walked next to Naomi as she loudly declared that she had an announcement to make. The reception was being held at her mother's house, and even though Jeff had learned that Melvin wasn't his son, he'd come in support of Damien.

"I have an announcement to make, so please quiet down!" Naomi's assertive tone got the people's attention. "As you all may know,

I've always told Jeff here that Melvin was his son. Well, as it turns out, I've been keeping a secret for all these years and Jeff just found out the truth, so I want to share it with you. Melvin was not Jeff's son." Pointing at the familiar man standing next to her, Naomi shocked the crowd. "Jeff was Lonnie's son." There wasn't a quiet person in the room at that moment. It was then that Jeff realized that Naomi had pulled a similar stunt as the one she'd pulled when she pretended to miscarry his baby, all the while, giving birth to Harvey's baby.

Jeff stormed out of the house with Naomi in pursuit of him. She was eerily calm as she pursued Jeff while telling him how Melvin had come to be. As it turns out, just as Carla had told Jeff some years back, Naomi had gotten pregnant by her ex, Lonnie. Lonnie didn't want the baby, so after a week of telling Lonnie about her pregnancy, Naomi told Lonnie that she'd miscarried the child. At that time, Jeff was married to Brianna and Naomi was Jeff's mistress. She saw her pregnancy as her opportunity to take Jeff from his wife once and for all. She knew the entire time that Melvin wasn't Jeff's son, but she used him to finish off Jeff's marriage to Brianna. However, Naomi had convinced Carla that she'd miscarried the child when she hadn't. To make her story believable, Naomi claimed to had been four months pregnant, when in truth, she was only three weeks pregnant when she'd pretended to have the miscarriage. This was to ensure that no one, including Carla, would suspect that the baby she was carrying belonged to Lonnie. After all, no one knew she was seeing a married man, and once she'd revealed Jeff's identity, she wanted to make sure that no one would question the paternity of little Melvin.

As Jeff opened his car door, he looked at the hateful Naomi. By this time, she'd began to raise her voice and threaten Jeff. Before he closed his door, he spoke the words that sealed Naomi's fate. "I was a bad man to Brianna and I was a bad man to you. I wasn't there for my children and I've cried many nights about my decisions. But do you know what makes me better than you? I stayed out of my children's lives because I knew I wouldn't be a good influence on them. I knew their lives would be much better without me. You stayed in your children's lives and you fed Melvin that same spoonful of hatred that you've been eating with for years. I didn't kill Melvin. You did. You poisoned your son to death. You sent your son on a mission to destroy my life and he lost his life trying to do what you convinced him to do. So yes, you were there for Melvin all of his life, but as we can both see, you being there was not in his best interest. You can threaten me and you can go to every witch doctor in town to try to destroy me, but one thing you are going to find out is that no weapon formed against me shall prosper. I don't hate you, Naomi. I actually feel sorry for you because you've let hatred consume you, but I'm not gonna let it come anywhere near my heart. I'm gonna keep loving and praying for you regardless of what you do to me."

With that, Jeff closed his car's door and Naomi kicked his car as he pulled off. When she turned around, she saw Damien standing behind her with tears in his eyes. "I knew you were evil, but I guess I underestimated how evil you were. By the way, Momma, you are responsible for Melvin's death. You're the one who sent him there to set that man up, so if you want to see his real killer, go look in the mirror. I'll go clean it off for you." Melvin then rushed back into the house. By this time, most of Naomi's family and friends were standing outside and staring at her. Many of them didn't know what to say or do. They'd seen how evil Naomi was, and because of this, everyone stood quietly and stared at her. "Let's go." A voice broke through the silence. It was Naomi's sister, Ravyn as she spoke with her children. After Ravyn left, many of the people at the reception began to leave. Naomi's mother, who was standing on the porch, turned around and went back into her house. When Naomi reentered the house, her mother turned around and rebuked her harshly. "You know, I did my best trying to raise you after your daddy left. Now, I wasn't the perfect mother by a long shot, but I did my best with what I knew. You knew better because I taught you better. You chose this life you're living and you've let hatred turn you into one ugly human being. Can't you see that it's killing you?! Are you really going to kill off your children and yourself just to get revenge against a man?! You chose this life, Naomi! You chose to play the whore, even when I told you that God was going to beat yo' behind! Now, you're reaping what you've sown! What amazes me about mothers like you is the devil can take your child's life, and you'll still keeping serving him! How much more does he have to take from you before you wake up and understand that the darkness you love hates you?! You walkin' round here blaming everybody for your troubles but yourself. Get out my house and don't come back here until you have Jesus! I gotta try to call some of these folks back so we can honor my grand-baby the right way since his own mother ain't got sense enough to act civilized... not even at her son's funeral. Leave and don't come back until you got Jesus with you! " Naomi's mother began to head to her bedroom, but she continued her verbal rebuke against her now humbled daughter. "Walkin' round here messing around with married men, and then, getting mad when they cheat on you! What did you expect?!" With that, Ms. Bloomfield slammed her bedroom.

Sensing his mother's pain, Damien came out of the den. "I'm sorry I was so hard on you. Can we just mourn my brother without the hatred?" Naomi nodded her head in affirmation as she wrapped her arms around her son. She let the tears fall as she held her son in the darkness. The daughter Naomi shared with Duke was no longer in her life. When Naomi and Duke divorced, Robin (Naomi and Duke's daughter, named after her sister Robyn) had requested to live with her father. As it turns out, Naomi was a competitive woman who didn't get along with women, including her daughter. Robin didn't come to Melvin's funeral because she was living with her father in Canada and the two wanted nothing to do with Naomi or her dysfunctional family. Henry, Naomi's son with Harvey, had come to the funeral, but he'd left immediately after the service.

The sound of Jeff's cellphone shattered the peace in his hotel room and scared him out of his sleep. It was Naomi's sister, Ravyn. Jeff tried to grab the phone from the nightstand, but he accidentally knocked it off the stand. Mumbling, Jeff leaned halfway off the bed and picked up his cell phone. Who could be calling him at one o'clock in the morning?

"Hello?"

"Jeff?"

"Yeah, it's me. Who's this?"

"Hey, Jeff. This is Ravyn."

"Ravyn?"

"I'm Naomi's sister. I'm sorry to call you so late, but I'm just getting filled in about the stuff my sister has been doing. First off, let me apologize for my part because I helped my sister conceal the birth of Harvey's son, Henry. That was my idea. I know it's old news, but I want to set the record straight. I'm Christian... believe it or not. When I reconnected with Naomi after Robyn's death, I had no idea that she was pregnant by your best friend. She told me that the baby was yours. She said that you didn't want any more kids and that you'd beat her up and cause her to have a miscarriage if you knew she was pregnant. I was afraid for my nephew's life. Naomi told me that Harvey was a cousin of hers (we have different fathers) and that he'd agreed to take little Henry in. She told me that you couldn't know about Henry because you'd probably hurt him, so that's why I let her come to Mexico to have the baby. If I had known what she was doing, I wouldn't have let her do it."

"That's okay.  Like you said, it's old news now.  I'm sorry we had to meet like this, but I want you to know that I am sincerely praying for Naomi and the rest of the family."

"Thank you.  And just know this... None of us knew that Melvin was Lonnie's son. I knew my sister was wild, but I didn't know that she was that wild.  I moved to Mexico some years ago after I'd given my life to the Lord.  I had to get away from my dysfunctional family.  I even stopped talking with my twin sister, Robyn, because of her ways.  A week before she died, she'd called me to say that she loved and missed me.  I should've known that something was wrong then."

"Oh wow.  That's terrible.  Well, I'm not trying to rush you or anything, but I've got to wake up in the morning."

"Oh, yeah... no problem.  I truly

understand. Well, I just wanted to call and apologize to you personally and just tell you to be encouraged."

"Thank you and it was very good meeting you. God bless you."

"God bless."

## Chapter 9

## Judgment Wears High Heels

Over the course of time, Naomi continued to spiral lower and lower into depression. She blamed herself for Melvin's death and she'd become consumed with hatred for Jeff. Damien had finally moved out and gotten his own apartment and most of her family wanted nothing to do with her. Three months after Melvin's death, Naomi met a well-known drug dealer whose street name was Muzzle through a mutual friend. Not only was Muzzle a dealer, but he was also a user. Naomi's initial attraction to Muzzle had everything to do with the fancy cars he drove and the extravagant lifestyle he lived, but it

wasn't long before Naomi began to
experiment with drugs. Six months after
meeting Muzzle and nine months after
Melvin's death, Naomi's body was found in a
parked car. She had overdosed on a cocktail
of cocaine, ecstasy and alcohol. The guilt
over Melvin's death was just too much for
her.

At Naomi's funeral, Jeff consoled his son,
Damien. Naomi's daughter with Duke
(Robin) also came to the funeral to pay her
last respects, along with her dad. Henry,
Naomi's son with Harvey stopped by as well,
but he wasn't accompanied by his father.
Instead, he'd come to the funeral with his
girlfriend and the two left immediately after
the funeral ended. Duke Jr. also came to the
funeral. Even though he wasn't Duke's
biological son, Duke had raised him as his
own. Duke Jr. didn't know that Duke wasn't
his biological father and Duke wanted to

keep it that way. When Duke Sr. saw Jeff at the funeral, he asked to speak with him and the two men went outside the church before the service started. Duke explained to Jeff that he didn't want to confuse his son and asked him to not reveal that he (Jeff) was Duke, Jr.'s real father. Jeff agreed. "Now's not the time for me to be selfish," explained Jeff. "I respect you for raising him and I see you've done a great job with him." The two men shook hands and reentered the church.

Krísi (Robyn's daughter) walked up to her aunt's casket and laid a flower across her chest. Krísi had grown up to be a very attractive (and seductive) young woman. She had her mother's curvaceous body and it was clear that her beauty had become her stronghold. Even though Krísi wasn't Duke's daughter with Robyn, she sat with Duke Sr. and Duke Jr. during the funeral. Behind Krísi sat her aunt Ravyn, the woman who'd raised her after her mother's death. Even though Ravyn had tried to raise Krísi in the Lord, she'd chosen to take the same dark path her mother once took. She'd decided to move to Los Angeles from Mexico because she loved the streets of Los Angeles.

Krísi was now the mother of a three year old little boy named Collin. Collin's father, Jacques, was in the process of trying to gain full custody of his son because, according to him, Krísi constantly exposed the young boy to different men. Jacques had already retained a lawyer and the court date was quickly approaching.

Jeff looked at his watch. He wanted to be there to support Damien, but he knew that some of the family would probably blame him for Naomi's death, so he didn't want to stay for the reception. "I can stay for the funeral, but I think it'll be a little awkward for me to show up at the reception. Especially after what happened last time," he said. Damien smiled at his dad and nodded his head. He had been amazingly calm at his mother's funeral. He'd shed a few tears, but he hadn't been the emotional wreck most of the family thought he'd be. "It's okay," he said. "I truly understand. Thank you for coming out to support me. It means a lot to me... Dad." Jeff hugged his son.

"You know I love you, right? And you know that if you ever need anything, I'm here for you. You can call me at any hour of the day or night."

"I know. I'll be okay. Can I tell you something without you judging me?"

"Yeah, sure; what's up?"

"I loved my mother... don't get me wrong, and I know I'm going to miss her. But I don't feel much of anything right now. I don't know if I'm still in shock or maybe the pain hasn't set in yet, but I just don't feel anything."

"That's normal. Like you said, you may be in shock. Either way, when you do feel something, call me and I'll help you through it."

"I think the problem is... and I hate to say this, but I feel like she died a long time ago. I grieved her life, so it's hard to grieve her death."

"Wow... that's deep. I don't know, but I do know that you'll be okay because you've got your father and I'll never walk out of your life again."

With that, Jeff hugged his son and held him tightly.


After the funeral was over, Jeff got a call from his newly separated daughter, Jessica. Rory had remained faithful for two years, but like Jeff said, the "fear of Jeff" would eventually wear off and he needed the fear of God to keep him. Rory's parents were ministers, but

Rory had chosen the wrong path.

Jessica called her father to arrange a lunch date with him since he was in town. Jeff agreed and they met up at a cozy outdoor restaurant called the Breezillian. When Jeff arrived at the Breezillian to meet his daughter, he was surprised to see how happy she was, especially given the fact that she'd just filed for divorce. Her daughter, London, was spending the weekend with Elijah and Brianna.

During lunch, Jessica excitedly told Jeff about the new home she was about to close on. No one knew that Jessica had been in the market for a house because she'd kept it a secret from everyone. Jessica had gone back to college, graduated and had just started working at a small law firm in town. Her husband, Rory, on the other hand, had opened his own barbershop a year prior to their separation. After years of struggling with his inner demons, Rory finally succumbed to temptation and had gotten another woman pregnant. His mistress miscarried the child, but the damage to Rory's marriage had already been done. Jessica filed for divorce and an unrepentant Rory decided to take advantage of his newfound singleness.

"How are you? Really."

"I'm good, Dad. Honestly, it hasn't been as hard as most folks think it has. I guess it's because I kinda expected this to happen. You know, I could tell that Rory wasn't ready to be a husband or father, so in a way, I've been preparing for this day for the last two years."

"I'm proud of you, Jessica. You could have let this thing destroy you, but you've chosen to take the high road. How's London?"

"She asks for her dad a lot, but I think

she's too young to understand now, so it doesn't bother her as long as she gets to see him."

"Do you need any money or anything?"

"Now, Dad. You know me better than that."

*Jeff laughed.* "Yeah, I forgot you are just like your mother... Ms. Independent Woman of the year."

"It's not like that. But Mom did tell me to never depend on a man to provide a place for me to stay, food on my table or clothes on my back. She always said you should never give another human being the power to determine if you ate or not."

"That's great advice. Yeah, she's always been a strong woman. I guess that's why I was so intimidated by her."

"You? Intimidated?"

"Yeah, believe it or not, men are easily intimidated by a woman who knows who she is and what she wants. When I was married to your mother, she would never ask me for anything. I respected her in my own sick way. It's funny, but when I left, I kept expecting to get a bunch of phone calls from her begging me to come back. I never got them. She filed for divorce a week after I left and I just couldn't face her."

"Yeah, sometimes, I wonder how Rory feels about me. Does he regret what he's done? Does he miss me?"

"He does... trust me. The problem is he's got more selfishness than he has love and when a man is more selfish than he is loving, he will always turn his back on the most important things in his life. He has a lot of foolishness in his system that he needs to get out. He's gonna have to go and experiment with a lot of women before he realizes how unique and valuable you are. For example, I've been with a lot of women, but I have yet to meet a woman as unique as your mother. She's one of a kind, but when I had her, I didn't know this because to me, she was just another woman. Do you want Rory back? You can be honest with me."

"Honestly... no. I'm too scared of him to take him back. I know what he's capable of. I remember the first day he opened his barbershop. He called me and said he was spending the night at the shop because he needed to make sure it was ready for the grand opening the next day. I cried that whole night. I knew what Rory was doing. When he came home the next day, he smelled like cheap perfume. We argued, I cried, but when I saw London crying, I remembered being like London. I used to cry when you and Mom fought and I didn't want her to experience that."

"I'm so, so sorry about that..."

"No, it's no problem. I've forgiven you, but I wanted to share with you that everything that happened with you and Mom wasn't all bad. It helped me to realize that I want more than to just be somebody's wife. I want to be happy, loved, respected and wanted. I don't want to share my husband and I don't want to feel like I'm not good enough. When I found out that Rory was cheating again, I started saving more money. I had an account that he knew nothing of. I started it two years ago after I'd found out about his affairs. For two years, I prepared myself emotionally, spiritually and financially for the day I'd become a single mother. I don't have any tears left to cry for Rory. Jesus is my knight in shining armor and He rescued me from that terrible marriage. I've made up my mind to just enjoy single living until God sends me the husband He has for me."

"You are really your mother's child and I thank God for blessing me with the opportunity to call you my daughter. You will be okay and Daddy will be here for you whenever you need me."

"Thanks, Dad."

"You're welcome, baby. I'd like to introduce you to someone very special to me. She should be here in a few minutes."

"Tahir, right?"

"Yes. She's a very special woman to me and I love her. I want to get your opinion about her because I'm thinking about proposing."

"What? Wow, Dad... Congratulations! I'm so happy for you."

"Well, don't be happy unless you approve of her. Your opinion is valuable to me.

A few minutes later, Tahir made her way over to the table where Jeff and Jessica were seated. She was a beautiful, Godly woman who obviously loved Jeff. Tahir was a dark-complexioned woman with smooth skin and deep brown eyes. Her thin physique and strong features made her look like a model who'd step right off the cover of a magazine. The two women talked about God and Jeff for more than two hours. They were definitely kindred spirits. When Jessica stood up to leave, she waited for Tahir to look away and she gave her father a thumbs-up. "She's the one," she whispered before walking away.

Meanwhile, on the other side of town, Rory was in his barbershop about to close it down for the evening. It was a Sunday evening and business was slow, so Rory decided to close the shop thirty minutes early because he wanted go home and watch a football game that he'd bet on. Across the street from

Rory's shop, stood a woman wearing red high heels, a short black skirt and a white midriff top. The shapely figure made her way towards Rory's shop.

Rory heard the bells on the door. "We're closed," he said. Just as he spoke those words, he looked up and beheld the most beautiful woman he'd ever seen. Her beautiful skin looked like melted gold. Her plump, red lips accented her bedroom eyes and her long, black hair flowed down her back. The beautiful young woman had a little boy with her, but Rory didn't pay much attention to the young man. He was smitten with the exotic beauty. There was no way that he was going to let her leave his shop without getting her phone number. "We're back open for business," he said, dusting off his barber's chair. The beautiful seductress smiled at him.

"I'm sorry we came so late, but this is my

son, and as you can see, he needs a haircut badly."

"No problem. Have a seat over here, little man."

"By the way, my name is Rory and if I can be unprofessional for a moment, I'd just like to tell you that you are the most beautiful woman I've ever laid eyes on."

"Thank you. You're not so bad on the eyes yourself."

"Well, beautiful lady... I'd love to get to know you better. Can I call you sometime?"

"Yes, you may. Do you have something to write my number down with?"

"Sure, I've got a pen right here. I've told you my name. What's your name and where are you from?"

"My name is Krísi and I've just moved here from Mexico."

Rory smiled and gently took Krísi's number

as she handed it to him.  Little did he know, the word "krísi" is the feminine translation of the Greek word for "judgment".

*"For the lips of a forbidden woman drip honey, and her speech is smoother than oil, but in the end she is bitter as wormwood, sharp as a two-edged sword. Her feet go down to death; her steps follow the path to Sheol; she does not ponder the path of life; her ways wander, and she does not know it."*

(Proverbs 5:3-6/ ESV)

# Chapter 10

## When Love Has the Mic

Five years had past since Jeff married Tahir. The couple had relocated back to Los Angeles, California where Jeff started his own sales and marketing company. Tahir started her own cosmetics line and was in the process of having her formulas patented. The couple was very happy and very much active in ministry. Jeff loved Tahir in a way that he'd never loved another woman, and he'd often brag about her to anyone who would listen. He'd never cheated on Tahir and he'd made up his mind that he would never cheat on her.

Jeff and Tahir had become close friends of Elijah and Brianna. Brianna was a modest woman who loved simple, but elegant hairstyles and little to no makeup. She didn't like to stand out. Tahir, on the other hand, was very much into fashion, so anytime Brianna didn't know what to wear to an event, Tahir would excitedly volunteer to accompany her on a shopping trip. Tahir was always looking for an excuse to shop and Jeff loved that about her, even though he'd often joke about setting her credit cards on fire. The couples enjoyed one another's company and Jeff's children enjoyed the closeness their parents had.

Jessica was engaged to her new fiance, Andrew, and the couple were planning to wed in the following weeks. Andrew, as it turns out, seemed to be the perfect mix of Jeff and Elijah. He'd been a man once consumed by the lusts of this world, and he'd almost lost his life after being caught in bed with another man's wife. After being shot by the husband of his lover, Andrew survived a coma that he'd been in for two weeks. Once he awoke from the coma, Andrew began to turn his life around. Seven years later, he was the pastor of a growing church in El Segundo, California. He met Jessica at a conference that both he and her stepfather had spoken at. The minute he laid eyes on her, he said he knew she was his God-appointed wife. Andrew was a faithful man and he accredited his faith to being grateful to God for giving him a second chance.

Jessica was still working at the same law firm that hired her more than five years ago. London, Jessica and Rory's daughter, was now six years old. Rory hadn't been in his daughter's life for more than four years. He'd lost his barbershop and it was rumored that he'd moved to Atlanta to live with a woman he'd met on the internet.

Elijah's church was preparing to host its annual Men's Day Conference that following Sunday and Elijah had listed Jeff as one of the speakers at the conference. Jeff wasn't too comfortable with the idea of speaking in front of more than thirty thousand people, but Elijah assured him that he'd "preach everyone under their seats."

The women from the church had an event planned as well. They were hosting their annual Women's Day Conference in the left wing of the church and Brianna was listed as the main speaker. Everything was going perfectly and everyone was happy.

Sunday finally arrived and the church was packed with hungry souls waiting to praise the Lord and hear a Word from Heaven. Jeff sat in the conference room nervously awaiting his time to speak. He'd just been led to the room to prep himself because he was the next featured speaker. Jeff knew what his sermon would be about; he just worried that he wouldn't be able to deliver it without stumbling over his words.

On the other side of the sanctuary, Tahir encouraged Brianna as she prepared to speak. "You look beautiful!" said Tahir. "Just wait until Elijah sees you." Brianna smiled. Tahir had turned out to be a great friend after all. Initially, Brianna had worried that the two wouldn't be able to be close because she had a history with Jeff, but Tahir proved her wrong. She was a confident, beautiful woman whose inner beauty surpassed her outer beauty. "Thanks. Well, I have this wonderful fashionable friend who won't let me step out the door looking any kind of way." The women laughed. At that moment, Brianna felt a love for Tahir that she could not understand. Tahir was her sister in the Lord and she was happy that out of all the women Jeff could have married, he'd chosen Tahir. "I really thank God for you, Tahir. I mean that with my whole heart. I love you like a sister and it amazes me that God favored me so well that He sent you to be my friend and sister in the Lord." Tahir smiled and dropped her head. "You always do this, you know? You always wait until I put my makeup on, and then, you make me cry. I love you too and I thank God for you. You have received me with open arms since the day I met you and I just want you to know that I genuinely love you like a sister." Suddenly, the women heard a squeal. They turned around just in time to see Jessica smiling at them with tears in her eyes. "Aw!!! Group hug!" she exclaimed to the now startled women.

It was Jeff's time to speak and a calmness had

taken the place of his fears. After his introduction, Jeff grabbed the microphone and looked at the floor for a few seconds before lifting his head to speak.

The room was filled with inquisitive men of all ages... men from all walks of life. Jeff began to preach about the adulterous man and the adulteress sent to ensnare him. The depth of his teachings wowed almost everyone in the auditorium, including Pastor Elijah. Jeff spoke from his heart and he passionately taught the men the value of having one wife versus having one or more immoral women. At the end of Jeff's sermon, many of the men had taken pages of notes and more than half of the men in the auditorium had been reduced to tears. Some of them were trying to figure out how to fix their broken marriages. They were confident that they now had the tools and the knowledge to repair the damage done to their marriages by pride, lack of knowledge and adultery.

Jeff asked every man in the midst of adultery to denounce his mistress or mistresses and to recommit himself to his wife, regardless of how imperfect his wife was. "God sent her so the two of you could build together, but Satan sent the adulteress to tear down what the two of you have built together because he's afraid of a united front!" Jeff's voice echoed throughout the room with power. The ushers began to walk through the aisles. "The ushers are about to give you all a piece of paper and a pen. You'll notice that the paper has already been folded up for you. I want each and every last one of you to take one of those pieces of paper, unfold it and list the names of your mistresses... past or present. I want you to even list the names of the women you've thought about cheating with and the women who are trying to

seduce you into cheating on your wives.
Don't write your name on the paper and
don't write the last names of the women...
just write their first names. I don't care if
you've been faithful to your wife, you need to
write something down because every last
one of us in this room has been tempted by
the adulteress spirit, whether we want to
admit it or not. At the same time, there are
some of you who likely won't write anything
because you don't want to let the adulteress
go. I say to you today that if you don't
release that woman, she is going to finish her
assignment and destroy your marriage. Once
your favor is gone, the enemy will begin to
blind and consume you until you are no more
or you repent and keep what's left of you. If
you're sitting next to someone like your
father-in-law, brother-in-law or someone
affiliated with your wife, I want you to stand
up and go into the aisles. Now, listen... if you
are the father-in-law, brother-in-law or the

wife's best-friend's husband, don't go running back to the wife insinuating that her husband was cheating. You don't know what he's writing down, but I want to make sure that every man in this room is set free today. I don't want anyone to leave here bound just because they're afraid to be honest. Even if you don't have any names to write down, if you are seated next to someone who is personally affiliated with your wife, step into the aisles right now and write the names of the adulteresses or temptresses Satan has sent your way. Don't worry. We're not going to read any of the names. We are about to bring them to the altar since many of these women will never see the altar of a church and we are going to pray for them with one voice." Jeff then turned to the main camera and spoke to the millions of viewers who were watching the conference from around the world. "If you are one of the many men seated at home, you can participate in this exercise too. Write down the names of any and every mistress you've had, every seductress who's seduced you and every temptress who is tempting you. Now, make sure your wife's not in the room because we don't want to end any marriages. Take the paper and lay it in front of you and when we begin to pray, I want you to stretch one hand towards that paper and the other towards your television screen. We are about to arrest and annihilate the spirit of adultery in many of your lives. Watch God work!"

By this time, almost every man in the room was writing on the paper that the ushers had given them. Many men were standing in the aisles, and there were a few men who weren't writing anything. The ushers made their way to the rebellious few and insisted that they write something down and they all did. After they were finished, Jeff had every man to fold the paper he was holding and each row of men was led to the front of the church to drop their mistresses' or temptresses' name into the two huge collection boxes at the front of the church.

After everyone was finally seated, Jeff had the men to stand and stretch their hands towards the two boxes. With one voice, they all began to tear down the spirit of adultery and cancel every demonic attack sent out against their marriages. Some of the men wept; some spoke in the tongues of angels, and others fell out under the power of God. Not one soul in that room was left unchanged.

After Jeff concluded his sermon, a teary-eyed Elijah made his way back to the podium. He was speechless. "I'm going to close on that note," he said. "Nothing else needs to be said. I believe God used this powerful vessel of His to restore and strengthen the marriages of every man who is seated in this room, and the millions who are watching today." After Elijah gave his closing speech, he asked for every man who needed prayer to make his way to the front of the church. He then asked Jeff to help him pray for the people. Jeff was to pray for the men coming from the left side of the room, while Pastor Elijah prayed for the men coming from the right side of the room.

As they began to pray for the men, Jeff knew that his life and his hardships hadn't been in vain. Sure, he'd done a lot of wicked things in his life, but God had forgiven him. He could now take the lessons he learned and help others avoid the paths he'd taken.

There were a few men left in Jeff's line, and he was simply amazed at what God had done in that conference. Jeff stood in front of one man, and just as the ushers were positioning themselves to catch the young man in case he was to fall, Jeff looked up. Standing in front of Jeff was a familiar, but teary face. It was Rory. It was obvious that his soul had taken a beating and he was about ready to give up on life. The bags under his eyes told a story of heartache, betrayal and regret... a story that Jeff knew all too much. "Lift your hands," said Jeff. After Rory lifted his hands, Jeff reached out and hugged him so tightly that he began to weep loudly. The pain in Rory was great. He'd been hurt and he was full of self pity, unforgiveness and regret. "Release it," Jeff said repeatedly as Rory continued to cry out. "Let it go, man of God! God forgives you. Let it go!" For a minute, it seemed as if Rory could not let go of whatever he was holding on to, but without warning, he finally broke and he too fell out under the power of God.

That night marked a shift in many homes

across America. Men and women were both set free and marriages were restored. Millions of demons were put to flight, never to return to the people and marriages they once called home.

- Jeff and Tahir continued their friendship with Pastor Elijah and Brianna, and Jeff eventually entered ministry full time. They all remained great friends for the duration of their lives.
- Jessica married her fiance, and the two went on to have two more children. Jessica and her husband eventually opened their own law firm and they became two of the most successful lawyers in Los Angeles.
- Jeff Jr. finished medical school. He went on to marry his high school sweetheart and the two remained married for the rest of their lives. They

had three children together.

- Rory's path back to God was a bumpy one because temptation continued to stalk and oppress him, but Rory was determined to take his life back and he did. After the conference, Rory was a new man and he decided to go back to school. He eventually met and married a woman from his father's church and he remained faithful to her, but she was not faithful to him. That marriage ended, but Rory didn't let it sour him. Three years later, he met and married the love of his life... a beautiful and intelligent woman by the name of Avianna. The two went on to have three children, and Rory eventually wrote two best-selling books about his experiences with the spirit of the adulteress.

- Damien went on to finish college and he remained close to his father. He became a Certified Public Accountant, and because he wanted to sever ties with his dysfunctional family (on his mother's side), Damien moved to New York. There, he met a woman named Janet and the two moved in together. It wasn't long before Damien realized that Janet was a lot like his mother. He eventually left Janet and moved to Georgia to put some distance between himself and Janet. He eventually gave his life to Christ and he met and married a woman by the name of Yvette. The couple had three children and Jeff was very involved in his grand children's lives.

- Carla went on to marry another man she'd seduced, but it was in that marriage that she met her match. Her husband, Quinton, was an abusive man who turned out to be schizophrenic. Carla remained married to him for more than fourteen years. She eventually fled her marriage in the middle of the night after her husband had beaten her and tied her up to a heater in the home. At the abuse shelter, Carla met a woman named Ulani who taught her about God. Carla eventually gave her life to the Lord and accepted the call of evangelism on her life. Today, Carla is an advocate for abused women.

- Krísi continued to seduce and ensnare men. She eventually met and married her judgment and the husband she'd chosen for herself (Frank) shot her after catching her in bed with another man. Krísi didn't die, but she was paralyzed from the waist down. Krísi never gave her life to the Lord.

- No one ever heard from Harvey or his son, Henry after Naomi's funeral. Harvey intentionally stayed off everyone's radar, even though he continued to live in Los Angeles, California. Harvey ended up marrying and divorcing three times before he gave up on women altogether.

*"Wisdom will save you from the immoral woman, from the seductive words of the promiscuous woman."*
(Galatians 5:19-24/ NLT)

# Character Review

**Jeff-** Jeff was a typical sinner. He saw women as disposable sex toys. He didn't mind committing to women in marriage, but he had trouble honoring the marriage vows. Jeff enjoyed the pleasures of this world, and because of this, he abandoned the (Godly) wife of his youth to pursue ungodly women. Jeff was mesmerized by what he could see, but oblivious to the demons he could not see. It wasn't until Jeff came across a woman more evil and conniving than himself that he saw the error of his ways.

**Brianna-** Brianna was Jeff's first wife. She was the woman who genuinely loved Jeff, but

Jeff did not love her because he did not know or love God. God is love, and therefore, without Him, Jeff was incapable of loving anyone... including himself. Jeff divorced Brianna to marry Naomi, but Jeff didn't realize that Naomi was judgment manifested in the flesh.

**Naomi-** Naomi was an adulteress who seduced, pursued and entangled Jeff in a web of deception so intricate that he could only be freed by the hands of God. Naomi had gotten pregnant with Melvin while she was sleeping with Jeff as well as her ex, Lonnie. When Naomi discovered that she was pregnant, she'd first told Lonnie, but he didn't want the child, so she pretended to have miscarried her son. She then told Jeff that she was pregnant by him because she wanted Jeff to leave his wife, Brianna. It worked. Jeff abandoned and divorced his wife to marry Naomi. Not only had Naomi deceived Jeff into thinking that Melvin was his son, she'd cheated on Jeff with his best friend, Harvey. As a result of her affair, Naomi conceived a son with Harvey and gave the child over to Harvey to raise. She'd then told her husband, Jeff, that she'd miscarried their child, when in truth, the child she had been carrying was very much alive.

**Carla-** Carla was Naomi's former best-friend. Carla envied her friend and was captivated by her life, so she pursued Naomi by pursuing Naomi's husband. Carla was more interested in Naomi's life than she was in Jeff, himself.

**Harvey-** Harvey was a typical playboy whose selfishness superseded that of the man he was mentoring (Jeff). A successful man himself, Harvey was not the happy, confident playboy he'd pretended to be. Instead, Harvey envied Jeff's life, and when he saw the opportunity to take something from Jeff, he took advantage of it. Harvey ended up raising his son, Henry, and after Jeff's marriage to Naomi ended, Harvey ceased all contact with Jeff. Hoping to get Naomi for himself and to continue hiding his dirty secret, Harvey convinced Naomi to get Jeff to sign over his parental rights to Melvin and Damien.

**Elijah-** Elijah, the son of a prominent pastor, was Brianna's second husband. A good and godly man, Elijah raised Brianna's two children, Jessica and Jeff Jr. as his own. He also fathered three children with Brianna (Ezra, Lily and Miles).

**Melvin-** Melvin thought he was Jeff's son. He was the first son of Naomi... the child Naomi used to coerce Jeff into divorcing his wife, Brianna. Because of Naomi's hatred towards Jeff, she'd poisoned Melvin's mind against the man he thought was his father.  In Melvin's attempt to exact revenge against Jeff, he'd lost his life in a car wreck.

**Damien-** Damien was Jeff's son with Naomi. Even though his father had abandoned him, Damien found it in his heart to forgive him. Even though his mother had attempted to poison his mind against his father, Damien chose to forgive and embrace him.

**Jessica-** Jessica was Jeff's first child with Brianna.  She met and married Rory, but her marriage ended when Rory found himself wrestling with the same demons her father had wrestled with.  Jessica had one daughter with Rory, whom she named London.  In the end, Jessica found herself about to be married to her God-appointed husband, Andrew, and we can safely assume that they lived happily together for the rest of their lives.

**Jeff Jr.-** Not much is said of Jeff Jr., but what we do know is that he went to medical school and he is Jeff Sr.'s second child.

**Robyn-** Robyn, like her sister, Naomi, was an adulteress who seduced men to get what she wanted. She'd married a man named Duke, and then, convinced him to use the money he'd gotten in a settlement to move to California. After their move to Los Angeles, Robyn began to pursue her sister's husband because she wanted to get revenge against her sister for abandoning her and her daughter, Krísi. After Robyn successfully seduced Jeff, she'd conceived a son with Jeff who she named Duke Jr., after her current husband. Robyn's secret came to light when her husband, Duke, hired a private investigator to follow her. After her affair was discovered, Duke went to the hotel room where his wife would meet her lover, Jeff, and confronted her after Jeff left. Panicked,

Robyn left the hotel and ended up dying in a car accident.

**Duke-** Duke was Robyn's husband who'd found himself tangled up in the web of deception that was crafted by his wife. After discovering his wife's affair, Duke confronted her, and the panicked Robyn left the hotel and died in a car wreck. After Robyn's death, Duke discovered that the man his wife had been sleeping with was her sister, Naomi's husband. Duke told Naomi, but Naomi convinced him to not confront her husband about the affair. Duke and Naomi eventually grew closer and started an affair of their own. Once Naomi left Jeff, she married Duke and the couple had a daughter that they named Robin, after Naomi's deceased sister and Duke's former wife, Robin. Once Duke and Naomi divorced, Duke took custody of Robin and he maintained custody of Jeff's son, Duke Jr.

**Ravyn-** Ravyn was Robyn's twin sister. She lived in Mexico because Ravyn wanted to put as much distance between herself and her dysfunctional family as possible. Deceived by her sister, Naomi, Ravyn helped Naomi to conceal the birth of her son, Henry. She also got custody of Robyn's older daughter, Krísi, after Robyn died.

**Krísi-** Krísi was Robyn's beautiful and seductive daughter. Much like her mother, Krísi used her beauty, form and sexuality to entice men into giving her what she wanted. She is also the woman who walked in Rory's shop and exchanged numbers with him. Rory, of course, was the husband of Jessica. Krísi was the judgment that was sent to wake Rory up from his whorish slumber.

**Rory-** Rory was Jessica's unfaithful husband and the father of their daughter, London. He found himself about to be caught in a web of his own after a beautiful and seductive Krísi walked into his barbershop. No one knows what happened to Rory and Krísi, but it was clear in the end that Rory and Krísi were no longer an item and Rory had learned his lesson. He returned to God, and the vessel God used to initiate his return, ironically enough, was his ex-father in law... a man who'd walked a mile in his shoes and could understand his struggle. Rory was one of the few men who'd escaped the snare of the adulteress.

*"Now the works of the flesh are evident: sexual immorality, impurity, sensuality, idolatry, sorcery, enmity, strife, jealousy, fits of anger, rivalries, dissensions, divisions, envy, drunkenness, orgies, and things like these. I warn you, as I warned you before, that those who do such things will not inherit the kingdom of God.*

*But the fruit of the Spirit is love, joy, peace, patience, kindness, goodness, faithfulness, gentleness, self-control; against such things there is no law. And those who belong to Christ Jesus have crucified the flesh with its passions and desires."*

(Galatians 5:19-24/ ESV)

Made in the USA
Columbia, SC
18 May 2021

38194451R00122